CONSPIRACY IN MARRAKECH

CONSPIRACY IN MARRAKECH

K.C. Harding

Author: K.C. Harding
Cover design: Verónice Fernández
ISBN: 9781726869539
© K.C. Harding

This novel is a work of fiction. The names, characters and incidents portrayed in it are the work of the authors' imagination. Furthermore this is a book for adults only. It contains sexually explicit scenes and graphic language, which may be considered offensive by some readers. All sexual activity in this book is consensual and all sexually active characters are 18 years of age or older.

All rights are reserved under International Copyright Conventions. No part of this text may be reproduced, transmitted or downloaded without the written permission of the author.

ONE

Beth had always wanted to visit Marrakech in the spring, but unfortunately she never got the opportunity. For decades there had been other priorities, like work, children and health problems. She also had a husband, who wasn't too keen on traveling to a Muslim country. Whenever she raised the topic, he would remind her of the neighbor who went to Libya for work and told them it was hard to get a decent drink there. Libya wasn't Morocco, Beth would say, and besides, couldn't he lay off the booze for just a couple of weeks? Yes, it took some convincing, but when they were both retired and her health was back to normal, he finally gave in.

So now they were in Marrakech, the magical city at the foot of the Atlas Mountains. Back in Aylesbury they had signed up for a tour that started in Casablanca ten days ago and was going to end here in Marrakech in a couple of days. Their fellow travelers had turned out to be a fine bunch. Twenty-five Americans and seventeen Brits. One couldn't get along well with everybody of course, but they had grown quite fond of a couple from Manchester and another couple from Boston. The tour itself had been wonderful. From the old imperial cities of Rabat, Meknes and Fes they had gone south to the Sahara. They had stayed in a charming hotel near the sand dunes and also visited the film studios close to that town she had forgotten the name of. Gladiator was filmed there, the tour guide told them. One of her favorite films, with that hot Australian actor. Her husband had even made a joke about her crush on him, which told her that he too was enjoying their time in Morocco. Also thanks to, it had to be said, their wonderful tour leader Mary, who spoke Arabic and had lived in Morocco for almost ten years. Originally she was from Manhattan. Imagine that, Beth had said to John, moving from Manhattan to Morocco! As much as she liked visiting this country she could never, not in a million years, leave Aylesbury, let alone leave it for a life in a culture that was so different.

Anyway, they were in Marrakech now, the city she had always dreamed off. They were lucky too, because even though it was spring already and temperatures had risen drastically in the past few days, there was still a lot of snow on the Atlas Mountains. The contrast between the white mountains in the background and the palmtrees in the city was something Beth had never seen before.

This morning a local guide called Hassan showed them his city. They had followed him through the narrow streets like ducks in a row. On every street corner he would wait and hold his water bottle up in the air, so they could all keep an eye on him. The streets were packed. Locals going about their business, on foot, on motorbikes and sometimes they were even leading donkeys and mules through the alleyways. Add to that the other impressions, like smells, colors and sounds and it was all just magical to her.

After their visit to the Bahia palace Mary and Hassan had announced that they would go to a Berber pharmacy now, a place where they would get a presentation about the traditional medicine of the local people. Their friends from Manchester had rolled their eyes, but Mary had told them that they were not obliged to buy anything and at least they would be out of the heat for an hour or so. Besides, Mary had added, everybody would get a cup of tea.

'Another cup of mint tea most likely,' John whispered, but Beth had hushed him. She liked Mary and she liked mint tea too.

Following their guide Hassan they walked through the busy markets of the old town, the souks, but there was no time for them to shop. At some point the narrow streets opened up to a small and very pretty square, where Hassan stopped for a brief explanation.

'This is Rahba Lakdima or Place des Épices. Herbs Square, I guess you would say in English. This is where the slave market used to be. A hundred years ago, before the French came, it was still possible to buy a slave here. Can you imagine that?'

Beth looked around and tried to take it all in. This historical place and the way it was now, with carpets in all sizes and colors hanging from the red ocher facades. Berbers in traditional clothes were selling herbs, hats and what seemed like chameleons in wooden cages. Someone else had noticed them too and asked Hassan about them. The chameleons, he explained, served a very special purpose: when a woman suspected that her husband was unfaithful, she could buy one of the animals here and then go to a witch, who would make a fire and utter some magical spell. The witch would throw the chameleon on the fire and if it exploded the husband was cured and would never be unfaithful again.

'Oh, how cruel,' a woman from Florida said.
'What if it doesn't explode?' someone else asked.

'In that case the spell didn't work, Hassan said. 'The man will still be unfaithful.'

'It would be better to throw him on the fire,' a woman said.

Everybody laughed, including Hassan, who then suggested that they continue their walk. The group crossed the square and turned right into a dark alleyway, where the Berber pharmacy was located. They couldn't go in straight away, because another group was just leaving. Germans, Beth thought. Most of them seemed happy to be outside again and only a few had bought something. One lady held up a bar of soap, so her husband could smell it. Another woman said something to her friend. Beth didn't understand her, but she did pick up the word 'argan'. She had asked Mary about argan oil last night and she told her to wait until they were here, in the Berber pharmacy, where she could buy as much of this special oil as she wanted.

While they were waiting in the narrow street she noticed a huge, obese man sitting in a chair that was so big and heavily decorated that it resembled a throne. The man had a long beard and as she looked at him, Beth realized that he gave her the shivers. At the same time she was aware that Muslims with beards made everybody paranoid these days, so she decided to look away and put her thoughts aside. Best to enjoy her holidays to the fullest and not worry about those things!

Beth was wrong to doubt the fat man in the chair. He was no danger to them. He was the owner of the Berber pharmacy and needed the tourists to make a living. He was happy they were here. Hassan had called him earlier to tell him that he was going to bring forty-two Brits and Americans and they had reminded each other that especially the Americans were good for business. They usually bought a lot of local products, where Europeans tended to be more cynical about these so called 'tourist traps'. So no, Beth didn't need to worry about the fat man. If she had looked behind her though, back to where they had come from, she would have seen another man, of average height and dressed in a burgundy djellaba, the traditional robe that so many people still wore in Morocco. A man hidden in the shadows, with the hood of his djellaba pulled up over his head. If she had seen him observing them she might have thought twice about entering the pharmacy. She didn't see him though and neither did any of the other members of their group. They were all too excited about their holidays, chatting, joking and laughing and waiting for the Germans to leave so they could go in. The man in the djellaba looked at them intently from his place in the shadows. Together with his associates he had planned this day meticulously. He watched and patiently waited until all of them were inside the building. Only then did he seem to breathe out and relax. He looked at the entrance of the shop for another minute before he turned around and disappeared into the maze of narrow streets.

 In the pharmacy Hassan the guide had just made a joke about Berber viagra and other herbs that could cure baldness, snoring, insomnia and basically everything else too, when the bomb went off. Beth and John were killed instantly and so were their friends from Boston and Manchester. Hassan the guide and Mary the tour leader never saw it coming either. Without knowing it, they had been standing just a foot away from the bomb that was hidden in a bag underneath the table in front of them. Twenty-nine of the forty-two tourists in the pharmacy got killed that morning. The thirteen that survived were almost all critically wounded. The explosion was devastating, sending shards of glass flying through the room and causing the ceiling to come down on those that had miraculously survived until then. Not only tourists died that morning. Six boys and girls who worked in the pharmacy for a very meager salary also didn't survive. The fat man did though. His throne was placed just at the right angle for him to escape the blast. He heard the explosion, saw the debris flying out into the street and felt a sharp pain in his cheek where a piece of glass had entered his flesh. But that, along with the destruction of his shop, was all for him.

The man in the burgundy djellaba was on the Djemaa el-Fna square when the bomb went off. He saw people look up in shock. The snake charmers stopped playing their flutes and tourists looked scared. The man got out his phone and dialed a number. When the other party answered, he said: 'Allah uh Akbar.' God is great.

TWO

The bar on the Southbank was packed with a crowd of young professionals that celebrated the end of another stressful week in the office. It was one of the hippest and coolest places in London, with a spectacular view of the river, Saint Paul's cathedral and the skyscrapers behind it. A bit older than most of the people here Katherine Davenport and her husband Roger Winfield were seated on a sofa in a corner, from where they had a good view on both the crowd and the lights of the city. Katherine, or Kate as most of her friends and family called her, had just come back from Zimbabwe. She had been there on a mission that turned out to be more dangerous than expected, so both of them were happy that she made it back to London safely.
'To a quiet month at home,' Roger said as he raised his glass.
Kate smiled, knowing perfectly well that it was very unlikely that the secret services would leave her alone for such a long time. Roger knew it too and more importantly, he had made his peace with it. A successful attorney in the City himself, it wasn't as if he was bored and lonely in times of her absence. They had been together for almost ten years and knew by now how to balance work and relationship.
Despite the dangers that came with it Kate loved her job. Her dad had always thought that life would bring

her something special and he was right. Even as a little girl she had always looked for adventure and danger. She had a privileged childhood in Essex, with plenty of money and luxury at home, but all she wanted to do as a little girl was play with boys and climb in trees. No dolls or dresses for her, but judo and karate and sparring with boys that were bigger and older than she was. It was only later, when she reached puberty, that she discovered she had a feminine side too. For the first time in her life she had let her thick, black hair grow long and even started to wear dresses every now and then. This to the delight of her mother of course, who had always disapproved of her tomboy side and fought many battles with her when she was little. Although she had passed away a long time ago, Kate remembered her clearly. Beautiful and strict, never a hair out of place and always dressed up as if she were expecting the Queen. It must have been her aristocratic, Lebanese blood, Kate often thought, or perhaps she was shaped by the events back in 1974, when she was sent to England by her parents, who knew that their country would be in turmoil soon. As the daughter of a well-known Christian aristocrat she had adapted to the upper class without a problem and by the time the civil war was over she was married with children and only went back to Lebanon to visit her family.

Roger smiled at her and said something, but the crowd around them was cheering and some men were slapping a young guy in a suit on the shoulder. Probably a promotion, she thought. Roger came closer and said: 'I think you have an admirer. Over there, at the bar.'

'Silly man,' she said, but she turned her head and saw a group of five young guys who were being cocky. One of them, a handsome, black guy did indeed throw her

some looks. Well, didn't he see that she was here with her husband? And how old was he anyway? Twenty-three? Still a kid, but not feeling like one, because now he even smiled at her. She picked up her drink and smiled back, but only briefly and not too obvious. Roger in the meantime seemed quite entertained by it all. Under the table she gave him a kick with her high heeled pump. Idiot, that meant, are we really in the mood for this? She had a jet lag and was still mentally recovering from the adventure in Zimbabwe. A flirt with a young guy was not what she needed right now. Or was it? She looked over at the guy again. One of his friends was talking to him now, but he clearly wasn't paying attention. While pretending to listen he looked at her and smiled again. What a cheeky young man, she thought, and sharply dressed too in his dark blue suit. Good body, good posture and a pleasant smile.
'What do you think?' her husband asked.
'I think you're a pervert, Roger Winfield.'
But she smiled and kissed him on the lips and again looked over at the black guy at the bar, who was still pretending to listen to his friend, but who had also seen the kiss and now seemed confused. Poor guy, what had he thought? That Roger was a colleague or just a friend? Perhaps she should show him her wedding ring? No, that might scare him off and she realized that she did feel like playing a bit more. She turned to Roger and said: 'I think I'll go get us another drink. What would you like? A glass of wine?'
Roger nodded with a goofy smile on his face. She got up and walked over to the bar, her hips swaying gently and her dark hair falling beautifully on her shoulders. Although she was a bit older than most women in the bar, she was easily the most striking. The exotic looks

that she had inherited from her mother, combined with the sexy dress and heels she was wearing tonight, made people look up and check her out. When she was younger the attention made her shy, but she had learned to embrace her femininity a long time ago and now felt comfortable with people noticing her presence. Comfortable as in not worrying about what others thought of her. Now, for instance, as she walked to the bar, she felt the eyes of at least five people on her, but she couldn't care less. The only reason she noticed was because it was part of her job, because she was trained to pay attention to her surroundings. Tonight though there was no danger, just a woman to her left who was shooting daggers at her and four men who were checking out her curves, one of them the guy who had smiled at her. She ordered two glasses of red wine and while the barman prepared them, she leaned on the bar and turned toward the black guy, who was standing just a few feet away from her. The guy didn't waste much time and gave her his best smile. Apparently no longer confused about the kiss, she thought. The fact that she had come over to where he was standing had given him his confidence back. Well, let's see what else he had. She raised her eyebrows, showing him that he had smiled enough and that it was time for him to step it up. He turned his head, quickly looking over at Roger, who was distracted by his phone, or more likely, was pretending to be distracted. Then he made his move and asked her if it was possible that he had seen her here before. She resisted making fun of this terrible pick-up line and said: 'I doubt it.'
To make things a bit easier for him she asked him if he was American or Canadian.
'American,' he said. 'From Washington D.C.'

Kate, who had been to the American capital on several occasions, mentioned some bars and restaurants that she remembered. The boy was clearly nervous underneath his cocky attitude, but started to relax now that they were talking about his hometown. Kate, in the meantime, made eye contact with Roger. No longer busy with his phone, he took a very keen interest in their conversation, even though he couldn't hear a word of it. It prompted Kate to grab the bull by the horns. While the boy was telling her that he and his family used to go to one of the restaurants that she had mentioned, she interrupted him and asked him why he had shown such an interest in her. His reaction was quite amusing. He coughed and stammered some words, without making any sense. But then he recollected himself and she thought, good for you, there is the man inside you stepping forward. Calmer now, he looked at her and asked if she was always this direct. She nodded and then surprised him again by asking if he wanted to join her and her husband at their table. Again he put his fist to his mouth and coughed, this decent young man from the United States.
'Your husband?'
'Don't worry about him. He is okay with it.'
'What do I tell my friends?'
'I'm sure you can think of something.'
With that she picked up the two glasses of wine from the bar and walked back to Roger.
'He is going to join us.'
Roger, knowing the drill, swapped seats and left the sofa for the chair on the other side of the table. Kate sat down on the sofa and watched the American come over. She patted her hand on the empty place next to her, basically telling him where to sit. Clearly still

nervous and uncomfortable he took a seat and put his beer on the table. Roger extended his hand and introduced himself.

'Roger. Kate's husband.'

'Will. From Washington D.C.'

'Nice to meet you, Will,' Roger said in a most pleasant tone of voice.

Kate nodded at his friends and asked him what he had told them.

'That I had met the two of you before at a birthday party.'

'At a birthday party even. You're a creative chap, Will.'

Will laughed, but was obviously not at ease yet with the whole situation. It crossed Kate's mind that he must be quite attracted to her to have gone so far out of his comfort zone to have joined her and her husband in this intimate corner of the bar.

'Look Will,' she said, 'we understand that you think this is all a bit strange, but really, let's just relax and chat a bit, okay?'

She smiled at him and Roger too showed the boy that there was nothing to worry about. Ever the conversationalist he asked: 'So D.C.? How are things there at the moment?'

And off the boy went, happy to be talking about his hometown again and this time Kate let him. Obviously it helped him relax and besides, Roger seemed genuinely interested. Her own thoughts though started to drift. First she noticed that dear Roger was more and more looking his age. He had turned forty a while ago, but his demanding job and short nights finally seemed to catch up on him. The wrinkles on his friendly face, the undeniable loss of hair, it was happening and it was normal, but still she felt for him. Then there was the

American, young, quite innocent still, but physically in his prime. The first time she had been to his city, she mused, he was still a child. It must have been fifteen years ago, just after university. First she had completed her Spanish studies, a year later International Relations. That summer her dad had surprised her with a ticket to the U.S. and enough money for a long road trip. Having passed on his solitary genes to her, he hadn't even asked her if she wanted to bring a friend. What he did suggest was that she visit his good friend Bob Delaney, a member of Congress for the Democratic Party. She stayed with him in D.C. for about a week. It wasn't the first time that they'd met, as Bob Delaney had frequently visited Essex in her childhood. However, it was the first time that they had talked like adults. Politics, ambitions, travel, life, they discussed it all. At the end of the week though she felt that she had spent enough time in his home. She bought a secondhand car and hit the road, driving south to Atlanta and New Orleans. It was after a great weekend in the Big Easy that she decided she wanted something different from her original plan. Las Vegas, Death Valley and California no longer appealed to her, so what she did instead was drive down to Mexico. When she called her parents a week later from Monterrey, her mother almost got a heart attack. Her dad said that he wasn't surprised at all, but when she told him that she planned to drive all the way to South America even he fell silent. She didn't make it to South America though, not that time. In Honduras her car got stolen in a violent robbery that put her in the hospital. Two guys on the side of the road had tricked her into stopping. One pulled a knife, the other picked up a baseball bat from behind a tree. Kate, who had been out of the car already, focused on the guy with the knife first. She had already had a black belt in judo and karate by then and managed to grab the guy's arm and dislocate his shoulder. She was too late for the other one though and the next thing she remembered was waking up with a splitting headache in a hospital in San Pedro Sula. Her car and money were gone and so was her desire to go further south. Her dad wired her money and when she was ready to leave the hospital she took a flight back to Washington D.C., where she spent another week talking to Bob Delaney. This time their conversations were of a different kind. Bob told her that she was not only bright, with a good academic basis too now, but that she also had something extra, something special that was much appreciated in certain government agencies. He was a bit vague at first, but yes, she was bright indeed and quickly understood that he was talking about the CIA. Things moved fast then. Bob made some calls, Kate met some people and before she knew it she was enrolled in a special program. She had loved it from the start. The military training, the sports, but also the psychology and the strategical way of thinking. Two years later, at the age of twenty-five, she was out on the street as an agent. She had worked for the CIA for more than five years, when she fell in love with Roger and realized that she wanted to move back home and do things differently. She left the CIA and went to work as an independent consultant. Before long both the CIA and MI6 hired her services on a regular basis, along with agencies from other countries. Bob Delaney still having her back and talking to people high up in both agencies, not because he liked her, but because he truly believed in her. Why? Well, while she was quite modest about her own skills, people in both agencies had repeatedly told her that she had what it took: intelligence and a good understanding of the balances of power. She was courageous too, they said. Prepared to take risks where others would back off. 'Add to that your looks and language skills,' Bob Delaney had said, 'and we've got ourselves the perfect spy.'

Looking at the American boy now she realized that she missed Bob. It had been ages since she had seen him. He was officially retired now, but still pulled at strings whenever it was necessary. Perhaps she could take her dad, who was retired too, for a few days to the U.S. soon. Well, she thought as she took a sip of her wine, that would be for later. Right now she was here in a bar with Roger and the young American, who seemed to feel more relaxed and was still chatting away with her husband. Perhaps it was time to reel him in? She looked at Roger and gave him a barely visible nod. Almost right away Roger excused himself and took his phone out of the pocket of his blazer. He got up and pressed it to his ear, heading for the exit of the bar. A lame excuse, Kate knew, but necessary to not spook the American too much. Now that she was alone with Will she turned her body more towards him and touched his muscular upper arm.

'Say Will, are you single or do you have a girlfriend back in America?'

Will blushed and said that he and his ex split up two months ago. Kate made the appropriate comments, playing the part of the older and caring friend, but she also crossed her long legs so that her nylons and patent leather court shoes were on full display for him. Most men were suckers for stockings and heels and she knew she had the legs to go with them. Sure enough Will let

his eyes wander right away. He did it quickly, in the hope that she wouldn't notice, but of course she did. Women almost always did. Very casually she shifted in her seat and got even closer to him. Her shoe was touching his trousers now and she moved her right hand gently up and down over her knee, her long, red nails on the sheer, black nylon. Again he looked, with the beginning of excitement in his eyes, but also still not sure what was going on.
'Tell me something, Will,' she began. 'When you first saw us sitting here, what did you think? That we were a couple or that we were just friends or colleagues?'
'I thought you were colleagues because most of the people here are.'
'What else did you think?'
'What do you mean?'
'Why did you look over? Not once or twice, but at least three or four times.'
'I thought you were beautiful,' he admitted.
'And available?'
'Yes.'
'You wanted to flirt?'
'Yes. I'm sorry. Like I said, I didn't know you were married.'
'Don't be sorry. We're here talking to each other because I like your attention. And so does Roger.'
'I'm not sure I understand.'
'I think you do,' Kate said and when the boy gave her a blank look, she added: 'We're one of those couples, Will. Kinky people who sometimes like to have fun.'
'Okay,' he said and then repeated that three more times. God, Kate thought, he really wasn't the sharpest knife in the drawer. He was a nice guy though and

goodlooking too, with his white teeth and soulful eyes, so yes, she was willing to take things a bit further.
'What I mean is that you can flirt with me. I like it.'
'And Roger?'
'He likes it too, in his own way. But forget about him for now. Focus on me and let's see if we can make it a fun evening. How does that sound?'
Reeling him in and wrapping him around her finger. Half an hour later, with Roger still gone, they were engaged in an intimate talk about relationships and love. It turned out that, despite his age and initial shyness, the American was quite eloquent. Kate found that she enjoyed talking to him, just like she enjoyed the proximity of his body and the seductive eye contact they frequently made now. It was clearly a matter of time before they would kiss. She crossed her legs the other way, right over left this time, and saw Will's eyes darting down again, drinking it all in. She laughed quietly and he asked her what was so funny.
'You seem to be taking a keen interest in my legs, young Will.'
She sat back, folding her arms across the chest and oozing a confidence that once again unbalanced the American. He stared at her briefly, but then laughed and nodded his head.
'Wow,' he said, 'you're quite something. And about your legs, they're spectacular.'
'Well, thank you, Will. What do you like about them?'
Inviting him to take a good look, which was exactly what he did.
'I love your calves,' he said. 'When you were walking away from the bar I noticed them first and wow, I could hardly believe it.'

'So you have been peeking at my legs quite a lot, haven't you?'
He nodded, but playing along with her now, not intimidated anymore. Then he reached out and put a hand on her knee. She didn't move or say anything, just looked at him. Slowly he started to caress her leg, down over her shin, up to her knee again and squeezing the beginning of her full, strong thigh. He moved forward and she did too and then they were kissing, tentative at first, but soon she could feel how the boy started to relax into it. As for Kate, she always loved this part. That first kiss with a stranger, knowing that she had her husband's permission. Exciting, bizarre and terribly kinky, it was all just up her street. And kissing with Will, it had to be said, didn't disappoint her at all. In contrary, the longer they kissed the more she liked it. Both had full and sensitive lips and now that the awkward phase was over the boy was passionate and intense. She wrapped her arms around his neck, pulling him closer to her. His upper body felt strong. She could tell that he worked out regularly. Meanwhile he continued to caress her legs, going up and down over her sheer nylons.
When Roger came back the boy didn't even notice. Kate did feel Roger's proximity and opened her eyes briefly, just long enough to make eye contact with him and confirm that he was all right and was enjoying this too. The look on his face was the look she had expected. Incredibly excited and hurt at the same time. The look had scared her all those years ago, when she had seen it for the first time, but that was then. Now she knew it was part of who he was and more importantly, she knew that this was what he truly enjoyed, even though it kind of hurt him too. In the

meantime Will was on the move with his hands. One was in her hair, while the other was on its way to her breasts. Slow down now, she thought, while she gently redirected him to her side. There was plenty of time for that later if all parties wanted it. But yes, where she hadn't been in the mood for this earlier on, she could now easily imagine taking the American home and into their bedroom.

Her job as a secret agent had a major influence on the kinky element of their marriage. At least one could say that it brought out the kink, because if it hadn't been for that assignment in Damascus, who knows, perhaps their relationship might never have moved out of vanilla territory. In Syria though things were turned pretty much upside down when she was assigned to work with a French agent, who was based in the Middle East and to whom she had felt terribly attracted. Freshly engaged to Roger she had really tried to behave, but a voice in her head kept saying that that was just not who she was. Engaged, about to be married and faithful, how uncomfortable she had always felt with those words! She was Kate, her inner voice reminded her, free, rebellious Kate who had always taken pleasure whenever she felt like it. Aware that she was being selfish though and possibly immature, she had continued to resist the advances of the French agent. However, at the end of the week they had drinks in a bar and then it happened. No love, no intimate talks, just passionate sex. Two bodies devouring each other, going at it for hours and hours. The next morning she felt entirely satisfied and terribly guilty at the same time. She had cheated on Roger and she was going to have to tell him. What also worried her was something that she finally had to face, something that would have become problematic for their relationship anyway. Sex with Roger was sweet and loving, but very much lacking in passion too. She didn't want to admit it at first, but just remembering the Frenchman's big, strong hands on her hips and his thick cock inside her set her on fire in a way that Roger never had. She wouldn't tell him that of course, but it was a problem that she needed to take into consideration. For some people mediocre sex might be a price they gladly paid in exchange for a loving partner, but that morning in the desert Kate knew that she wasn't one of them. She needed more, much more. At that moment she was convinced that the engagement would be over and that it was probably for the best too.

Back in London she and Roger had the conversation. Understandably he felt hurt and betrayed. They broke off the engagement and that was that, she thought. A week later however she found him on her doorstep with flowers. Flowers? Wasn't she the one who needed to apologize to him? Well, it turned out that he hadn't come to apologize, but to be more honest about what he felt. It was then that he told her that her affair turned him on immensely. At first she didn't believe him, thinking that he was just desperate to get her back, but they talked the whole night and she learned a lot about this strange kink of men getting pleasure out of being cuckolded. So apparently Roger was one of them. She asked him how long he had had this desire and he admitted that it stemmed from a time long before they met. That was good, she thought, because it meant that it was not directly linked to her affair.

After this emotional and revealing night they continued their relationship, but now with the promise that they would communicate better and be more open with each other. In the months that followed they also took their newly found knowledge to bed with them. During lovemaking she would tell him about the Frenchman and how well he had fucked her. It drove Roger wild and even though he never matched the Frenchman, or some of the other lovers she had, Kate got happier and happier about their sex life. They started to experiment in other ways too. She would tie him up and occasionally even spank him like a little boy. It was like opening the infamous Pandora's Box, both of them discovering more and more kinky games. At some point they switched roles too, him dominating her, but that just made them laugh, because somehow it felt ridiculous. It was clear for them then that it only worked when she was dominant and he was submissive.

In the years that followed they got married and bought a beautiful house near Holland Park. Roger was making a fortune and Kate had always had money. They seemed a rich, yet ordinary couple and in many ways that's exactly what they were. They had their group of friends and their careers, Roger working in the City, Kate at the Ministry of Foreign Affairs, which was a smokescreen of course and a perfect alibi for her secret missions. They never told anyone close to them about the kinky side of their marriage, but together they slipped in and out of that dark and delightful world whenever they felt like it. In the basement of their house they had created two playrooms full of kinky instruments, Kate's dungeon where Roger served her in ways that were incomprehensible to the vanilla world outside. They also played when Kate was traveling. That usually involved a chastity belt for Roger and a lover for Kate. One of them was the Frenchman with whom it had all started. She had never worked with him again, but whenever she was in the Middle East she called him up and sometimes they would spend the night. Sex with him remained spectacularly good, the difference with the first time being that now she could tell Roger beforehand. No more guilt, just pleasure and a twisted complicity with her husband.

And now they were here with young Will from America, who was kissing her and trying to feel her up while her husband was watching. They were all excited now. She could see it in their eyes and feel it in her body. Her panties were getting wet and her nipples were hard. Perhaps they could skip the dancing and the drinks and take the boy home right away. She broke off the kiss and suggested as much to both men, who of course agreed. Fifteen minutes later they were in a taxi driving across London. Roger in the front seat and she and Will in the backseat, where they continued their kissing. Here, in the dark, she allowed Will's hand to go further up her legs. She had positioned herself in such a way that Roger could see a bit of the action too. He was talking to the driver about cricket, facing the man, but glancing at them in the backseat from the corner of his eye. She spread her legs a bit wider, so that Will could work his way up and Roger wouldn't have to miss a thing. Will's hand went up indeed, over her stockings and to the bare skin above it. She lifted up her dress and pushed her hips forward. While Will slipped a finger underneath the lace panties and began to caress her wet cunt, she looked her husband straight in the eye. No more cricket talk for him. He was extremely excited, she could tell and so was she. His gaze went down to between her legs and stayed there, watching intently how his wife was getting fingered by a stranger. Oh, and how well Will was touching her clit! Gently and with just the right rhythm. She moaned softly and closed her eyes. She threw her head back and focused on the American's fingers that were about to bring her to a climax. It was then that her work phone rang. Both Roger and she recognized the ringtone immediately and knew that most likely young Will was about to be sent on his way. She took the phone out of her bag, still breathing hard, but trying to recollect herself as she sat up. As she had suspected it was her contact at MI6, who asked her if she had seen the news. A terrorist attack in Marrakech, many casualties, mostly American and British. It happened during the day, her contact said, and at first it had been total mayhem. Now a clearer picture emerged and to make a long story short, a car would swing by her house and take her to Gatwick Airport from where she would fly to Marrakech.

THREE

The next morning Kate woke up in her suite in the Mamounia hotel. As always MI6 had arranged everything perfectly. A driver had picked her from the airport and brought her to this luxurious five star hotel near the old medina of Marrakech. Exhausted from the night out, the wine and the sudden flight to Morocco she had checked in, gone to her room and fallen asleep before she could even send a message to Roger to tell him that she had arrived. This morning at breakfast she chatted with him briefly. He had taken Will's number, he said, and added that perhaps they could invite him over some day. Sure, Kate had replied, but truth was that the moment she was out of the country on a mission, she forgot almost everything about her life back home. Not her husband or her dad of course, but she could hardly care less about Will right now. Many people had died here yesterday in a vicious terrorist attack and she had come to figure out what happened exactly. After breakfast a meeting was planned with an agent from the DST, the Moroccan secret service and a CIA agent, who had been in the country already. People from the American and British embassies were supposed to be on their way down from Rabat as well and she would have to meet with them too. She also wanted to see where the attack took place, even though she could tell from photos in the

L'Économiste, the newspaper in front of her, that not much was left of the Berber pharmacy. Just rubble, chaos and dust. Nevertheless she wanted to go take a look for herself later today.

The newspaper mentioned that a suspect had been arrested. No doubt she would hear all about that later, but it was a good start at least. Five pages of the L'Économiste wrote about the attack. Kate's French was good enough to understand most of it. Some journalists were certain that it was a typical IS-attack and others speculated that Al Qaida had resurfaced. But yes, it was all just speculation. No one in the media knew who was responsible, not yet anyway. She expected that Islamic State would make the call at some point and claim the attack, but that too didn't mean so much anymore, as they claimed almost every attack nowadays, even when the culprit turned out to be mentally unstable and without much of a religious background.

As she finished her coffee she read through the rest of the newspaper. Stockmarket news, the upcoming concerts of Cindy Stones here in Marrakech, the opening of a new office tower in Casablanca, three pages of football news and at the very end the weather forecast. Hot temperatures in the day, cooler at night.

The Mamounia hotel was not only one of the best hotels in Morocco, it was also at walking distance from the legendary Jemaa el-Fna square and the ancient medina. A hotel since 1923, it had accommodated an impressive list of famous people. Actors, singers, heads of states and European royalty had all stayed here. One of the most famous guests had been Winston Churchill. He came to the Mamounia to paint and when he met

Franklin Roosevelt here in 1943 he told him that 'it was the most lovely spot in the whole world'. They must have been in the gardens when he said that, Kate thought, because as beautiful as the hotel itself was, the gardens were just breathtaking. After breakfast she had gone for a stroll and now she was sitting in the shade of a tree, drinking tea while she waited for the others. The Moroccan agent of the DST was the first to join her. He was a handsome and well dressed man with dark skin and brooding eyes, who introduced himself as Elias Ramzi. He spoke English to her and even though she could have answered him in fluent Arabic, she didn't. No need to show her hand yet, not unless it was necessary. They waited for the American and talked about the weather in the meantime. The CIA-man showed up five minutes later. He took a seat, loosened his tie and without further ado addressed the Moroccan agent in a somewhat agitated, even aggressive manner: 'So what happened? What do you know? And who have you arrested?'

Agent Ramzi didn't seem intimidated. He stood his ground and offered the American his hand.

'Elias Ramzi, DST. You must be Ben Mitchell.'

The American apologized then and admitted that he was stressed out and possibly even out of his depth. He had arrived in Marrakech two days ago to oversee the security surrounding the two concerts of Cindy Stones, the famous singer who was on a world tour. Of course the CIA would normally not worry about a pop artist, but Miss Stones got recently engaged to the son of the American president, so that changed the whole picture. In any case, when Ben Mitchell came to Morocco to make sure protection was in place for the upcoming visit, he hadn't expected to be confronted with a terror attack on a group of tourists.

'What a mess,' he sighed.

He was about fifty years old, Kate thought. Slightly overweight and with beads of sweat on his brow and upper lip, he didn't seem the kind of man who would easily adapt to a different and exotic culture. Ben Mitchell, she knew, was not the person the CIA would have sent if he hadn't been here on other business already. No, she was the one who was sent here, officially by MI6, but she was sure things had been discussed with their colleagues in Langley too.

'The bomb went off just before Friday prayer,' agent Ramzi said. 'Thirty-five people died, nineteen Americans, ten British and six Moroccans. At first we suspected that it was a suicide bomber, but we now know that the explosive had a detonator and was probably put in the room before the tourists came in. It went off when the group had been inside for about ten minutes.'

He looked at Kate who nodded and encouraged him to go on.

'Last night we arrested the perpetrator. A young man called Rachid Mansour. He is an employee of the pharmacy. He has worked there for three years. No priors, no ties with people and organizations we monitor, but some time before the tour group arrived he left the building. When we searched his apartment we found enough material to make another bomb. C-4, plastic binders, detonators, etc.'

'Has he confessed?' Ben Mitchell asked.

The Moroccan shook his head.

'He denied everything and stopped talking to us altogether when we continued to press him.'

'Where is he held?' Kate asked.

'In one of our buildings here in town.'

'I would like to see him.'

'Why?' the Moroccan asked. He looked her in the eye, with a hint of a disdainful smile playing around his mouth. Did he think of her as 'just a woman' or perhaps as a meddlesome outsider? Or did she imagine the disdain?

She switched to Arabic and told him that she had been sent here by her government to investigate the violent death of fellow countrymen. If the DST had arrested a suspect, she said, it was quite obvious that she needed to interrogate this man. She was sure Mister Ramzi understood and would do all he could to facilitate this interrogation.

The Moroccan looked at her without disdain now, she was sure of it. What a good dressing down in one's mother tongue could achieve!

'I'll do my best, Mrs. Davenport. You have my word. I do need to take it up with my superiors though.'

'Good,' Kate said, while she wondered why he couldn't have agreed the first time she had asked. She let it go though, not wanting to antagonize this local agent any further.

'Where did you learn to speak Arabic so well?' he asked.

'I have Lebanese roots,' she said. 'From my mother's side.'

'Are you a Muslim too?'

She shook her head.

'My grandparents were Lebanese Christians.'

'A pity,' he said, but sparks were dancing in his dark eyes. He seemed to look at her differently now that he knew that she spoke his language. She didn't want to encourage him any further though, so she switched her attention to Ben Mitchell.

'I understand that you and I are meeting people from our embassies at the British consulate.'

He looked at his watch and said: 'In less than two hours we're expected there.'

'Good. So I could perhaps meet the suspect afterwards. What do you say, mister Ramzi?'

The Moroccan nodded pensively.

'I'll try to get you clearance,' he said, 'but this is Morocco. Things move slow here.'

In the British consulate high officials from the United States, Great Britain and Morocco were gathered together. The ambassadors were there, together with their assistants. The mayor of Marrakech arrived just after Kate and Ben Mitchell, accompanied by police officers with lots of medals on their chests. Ben Mitchell immediately went over to his fellow countrymen, while Kate chatted to the British ambassador briefly, who told her that he had once met her father at a fundraiser in London. Most of the people present, she observed, were men. Everybody was dressed formally and she was glad that she too had changed into a dark gray suit and pumps before coming here.

After the small talk the people who mattered sat down at a conference table and closed the door. Introductions were made and a surreal hour of veiled threats, hollow promises and boring bureaucracy followed. Nothing that was said here, she realized, would help her in any way to get to the bottom of what happened yesterday, but she had put in an appearance and at least now knew who was who. When she left the consulate she called agent Ramzi to remind him that she wanted to interrogate the suspect. He said he was terribly sorry, but the best he could do was set up the encounter for tomorrow morning. Annoyed and feeling that precious time was wasted here, she took a taxi to the Mamounia hotel, where she changed back into her jeans and sneakers.

From the hotel she walked past the Koutoubia mosque to the Jemaa el-Fna square, a vast open space where dozens of stalls sold fresh orange juice and where snake charmers tried to get tourists to take photos of their cobras and vipers. The sound of their flutes floated over the square. Later at dusk, she had read, Jemaa el-Fna would really come to life. She looked forward to seeing it, but first she needed to find the Berber pharmacy where the bomb had gone off. Behind Jemaa el-Fna she walked into the maze of narrow streets that made up the souk, the market of the old town. It was her first time in Morocco, but she had seen plenty of souks in the Middle East. Walking past shops that sold olives and fruit, herbs and spices, exotic dresses or just ordinary things like toiletries and towels, she finally came to Rahba Lakdima, the Place des Épices, the square where the tour guide had stopped with his group to tell them about the chameleons and the unfaithful husbands. She crossed the square, just like the group had done, and looked up at the carpets hanging from the buildings. The atmosphere of this part of town reminded her of Mali, where she had been a couple of years ago. A taste of Sub Saharan Africa. She had to ask directions now, so she stopped an older man in his tracks, who told her to take a left turn and then, at the pottery, go right. Two minutes later she was looking at the ruins of what had once been the Berber pharmacy. She couldn't get really close, because the place was still swarming with police and firemen, but she felt she had done the right thing in coming here anyway. The bomb, she saw with her own eyes now, had been devastating. There was really no point in hoping to find any clues underneath the debris. Besides, it looked like the police had arrested the perpetrator anyway. Getting him to talk was more likely to lead them to possible accomplices than hanging around here. On the other hand, the suspect hadn't confessed yet and it was her job, more than anyone else's, to delve deeper and try to look at things from a different perspective. Sometimes she would still come to the same conclusion as the police, but there had been cases too in which her approach changed the outcome of the entire investigation. It was exactly because of that possibility that she was here now.

Kate turned around and went back to Rahba Lakdima, where she climbed the stairs of Café des Épices. She ordered a coffee when she passed the counter and went up another staircase that took her to the roof terrace. Looking out over the old medina, all roofs and minarets under a sky that was gradually becoming dark, she imagined the tour group's last day in Marrakech. They'd been on a cultural visit, people were saying. Where else did they go, she had asked at the meeting in the consulate. They had gone to the Saadian Tombs, she was told, and then to the Bahia palace and the souks, before coming here. The local guide had called the Berber pharmacy to let them know that he was bringing Americans. Was this a regular program, she wondered. Did tourists of this agency visit Marrakech on the same day every week? If so, they were an easy target for the suspect. It would have been a piece of cake for him to find out which nationality would come when exactly. She picked up her phone and called her contact in London to ask if they could confirm the agency's program. Her contact promised to call her back and as she sat there waiting, looking at her phone, another thought occurred to her. The police, agent Ramzi told her, had looked for the victims' phones in the rubble. Some were found and memory cards had been analyzed. Four of the tourists had taken photos when they entered the pharmacy, one man or woman had filmed it. Nothing interesting was found though, Elias Ramzi had assured her. Just images of jars full of herbs and smiles of people who were now dead. She believed him and wasn't so interested in those images anyway, because the bomb had most likely already been in place. She was thinking something else though: perhaps another tour group had visited the pharmacy just before the American/English group. And if so, what if someone in that group had taken pictures of the pharmacy? Perhaps something of interest could be found in them? It was a long shot of course, but this was exactly what she was hired for, so she felt determined to pursue this idea that was not even a lead yet. She picked up her phone again and called Elias Ramzi to ask him if he could find out about other groups. He would be on it right away, he said. Having done all she could for today she got up, paid her bill and went down to the square. It was getting dark quickly and true enough, the city became even more magical. The lights of the markets, the sounds and smells and the endless maze of narrow streets. She followed them back to Jemaa el-Fna square, where a massive crowd of tourists and locals had gathered. The sky was completely dark now. The only light came from the naked bulbs of maybe a hundred food stalls, from which smoke and the smell of food rose up. Groups of people gathered around artists too. Acrobats, medicine men who sold bones and spices and musicians with loud drums. It seemed as if a wild circus had come to town, but she had read that it was like this every night. Sitting on a bench of one of the food stalls she ate a harira soup and afterwards wandered around some more, taking it all in, the atmosphere of this crazy, legendary city.

Later, when she was almost back at the hotel, her contact in London called to tell her that yes indeed, the travel agency came to Marrakech the same day of each week. Same program too. She thanked the woman and dialed Roger's number. As they spoke about anything but their jobs, she walked into the garden of the hotel. It was even more beautiful at night, she told her husband. The buildings, the trees and plants and how they were all subtly lit. Then there was the pool, that almost didn't look like a pool, but something that was floating in front of her eyes. It all seemed to have come straight from a fairytale.
'It's like Arabian Nights', she said to Roger. 'We should come here together some day.'

FOUR

It turned out that the interrogation of the suspect couldn't take place in the morning after all. Kate spent some frustrating hours on the phone, talking to Elias Ramzi, her contact in London and the British ambassador. The suspect had been taken to another location, she was told, where he was interrogated by the Moroccan police. They would need to wait for them to return him to the DST.
Kate got the feeling that the Moroccans were stalling her. Local police or DST, neither wanted her to snoop around and she suspected that it had to do with their own, unconventional methods of interrogation.
It was half past twelve when she finally got the green light. Elias Ramzi picked her up in his Toyota Landcruiser and drove her to Gueliz, the new part of town which was home to boulevards, shopping centers and fancy restaurants. The building of the DST was located at a busy corner near the Jardin Majorelle, the garden that once belonged to the fashion designer Yves Saint Laurent.
Rachid Mansour, the suspect of the terror attack, turned out to be a young man of eighteen years old. He looked even younger, Kate thought, with his short, curly hair, skinny body and babyface. He also looked very frightened. One of his eyes was closed and bruised and Kate was certain that his body would carry more

signs of torture. Elias had told her in the car that the boy still denied all charges, let alone that he had given the DST and the police anything else to go on. They still didn't know, Elias said, if they were dealing with a loner or with a terror cell.

They were sitting opposite the boy, who had his arms tied to the chair he was sitting on. Elias began to ask him questions, intimidating him. Not asking him if he had done it, but who were his helpers, who had made the bomb for him, etc. Kate observed the boy's reactions and it was halfway the interrogation that she started to have doubts. She couldn't say why, but the boy's answers struck her as truthful. Apart from the fear in his eyes she saw something else too: astonishment and disbelief that he had ended up in this situation. Elias Ramzi continued his barrage of questions and accusations, but all the boy did was cower and stare at them with wide and desperate eyes. There was no point in continuing like this, she realized. Besides, this was her interrogation. Politely but firmly she told Elias that she would like to be alone with the suspect. Elias protested and said that for her safety it would be better if he stayed in the room with her, an argument so ridiculous that she didn't even warrant it with a reply. She just looked at him and said that she would see him outside in a minute. Reluctantly he got up and left the room, probably insulted, but well, so be it.

When she was alone with the boy the atmosphere changed. The boy relaxed a bit and she sat back in her chair, giving him a sense of space.

'If I smoked I would offer you a cigarette,' she said in Arabic.

'I don't smoke either,' Rachid replied.

'Good for you.'

He looked at her, still cautious, but with a trace of curiosity in his eyes too.

'So, Rachid,' she began, 'they say that you left the pharmacy a few minutes before the bomb went off. Why was that? What happened?'

'Someone came to the shop and told me that my mother was very sick, so I went home.'

'Who was this person?'

'A man I had never seen before, but he told me that he worked for the clinic in our neighbourhood and well, I was worried about my mother, so I didn't think about it much and just hurried home.'

'Where do you live?'

'Near Bab Doukkala.'

'Where is that? Far from the pharmacy?'

'No, it's the northwestern part of the medina. Near the busstation.'

'So you walked home?'

'Yes.'

'And when you got there your mother was fine?'

'She wasn't there and nor were my brother and sisters.'

'Where were they?'

'My brother was at work. He works at the Mandarin Oriental hotel. My mother and sisters were at the market. A neighbor told me I could find them there, so I ran over and discovered that they were all right.'

'How about your father? Is he still alive?'

'No,' the boy said, 'he died last year.'

'I'm sorry to hear that.'

The boy shrugged. He looked less scared now and seemed even eager to answer her questions.

'So what do you think happened?'

'What do you think? Someone framed me!'

'How about the things they found in your room?'
'I didn't know about that either. They told me that they found a box underneath my bed. They showed me a photo of it. I had never seen it before.'
What if the boy was telling the truth, Kate wondered.
'How long have you worked in the pharmacy?'
'Three years.'
'So you were what, fifteen, when you started there?'
He nodded.
'Do you like working there?'
'Yes, I love it.'
'Why?'
'The money I make, the tips I get sometimes and the foreigners I meet.'
'You don't hate them?'
'Why would I? Thanks to them I have got a job.'
'Okay,' Kate said, drumming her fingers on the table. 'Look, perhaps you can help me with something. I understand that these American groups come every week?'
'In the high season, yes.'
'Now it's the high season, right?'
'Yes.'
'So they were there last week too?'
'Yes, and the week before that.'
'Always with the same guide?'
'Yes. Hassan.'
'Did you know Hassan well?'
He shook his head and explained that Hassan brought clients, but they hardly ever spoke to each other. The employees of the pharmacy did the presentation and the selling and when the group moved on, Hassan would get his commission and leave.
'Did Hassan always come with Americans and English?'

'Yes, most of the time.'
'Do you work with other guides too?'
'Yes, of course. Hassan is just one of them.'
'Was. Hassan died. You know that, right?'
'Yes.'
'You're lucky, Rachid. If this unknown person hadn't told you that your mother was sick, you might have died in the explosion too.'
'I know, but now I'm here, arrested and sent to prison. That's not much better than dying, is it?'
She didn't answer him. She was thinking about what had occurred to her last night. The DST still hadn't come up with an answer, but perhaps Rachid knew.
'Rachid, tell me something. Was there a group before the American/British group? Do you remember?'
'Yes, of course I remember. That was Fatima's group. Germans.'
'Did they leave long before Hassan's group arrived?'
Rachid thought about that and shook his head.
'I'm not sure, because when the man came in to tell me about my mother, the Germans were just arriving. I was going to assist at the presentation for them, but I left before my colleague started. That's why I'm not sure how much time there was between the two groups.'
'Do you know which agency Fatima's group belonged to? Or perhaps you know where they are now?'
'No, sorry. I just know they were German.'
'Do you know Fatima's last name?'
'Nouri, I think.'
'Where can I find her? Do you have her number?'
He shook his head, but told her that she could try the association of local guides. Not having any further questions she thanked him, got up and left the room. While Elias Ramzi was busy talking to his colleagues,

she made a quick call to London, passing on the name of Fatima Nouri and asking them to please look up her phonenumber.

'I think he might have been framed,' she said to Elias when they were back on the street.
'By whom?' he asked.
'I don't know, but it seemed to me as if he was speaking the truth.'
'I doubt it. You don't know Moroccans. They are born liars when they are under pressure.'
'I'd like to check out his house. I understand if you have other things to do, so I can go alone too. I could take a taxi.'
'What do you expect to find there? We already searched the house and found everything we needed.'
'I know. Nevertheless, I want to check it out.'
'You are a stubborn woman, Mrs. Davenport.'
'I know I am, Elias.'
She could tell that she was making him nervous. He was probably not used to a woman who had unusual requests and demands and who was calling him by his first name now, but had not yet given him permission to do so too. Well, experience taught her that there was nothing wrong with keeping certain boundaries, even though it probably annoyed the hell out of this Moroccan man. Besides, she had given him an opening to go and leave her to it. He said that he had nothing better to do though and that he would accompany her to Rachid Mansour's house near Bab Doukkala, one of the ancient gates to the medina.

One of the sisters of Rachid Mansour let them in. Her eyes were red from crying. They were introduced to the mother and another sister, who were seated on one of the sofas in the living room. The brother was probably at work, Kate thought. The women were dressed in traditional kaftans, but didn't wear headscarves in their own home. The three of them were voluptuous women with wide hips and big bosoms and butts. The mother's hair was long and gray, the haircut of the sisters was more stylish. They were desperate for news about Rachid and implored them to please believe them when they said that he must be innocent.

'He simply must be,' one of the sisters repeated. Although Kate was inclined to believe her, she would have been a lousy agent if she had taken the women's word for it. Instead she asked the sister why she was so sure that her brother hadn't radicalized.

'Rachid loved working in the pharmacy, because it brought him in contact with western tourists. He liked to practice his English with them and often he would come home with enthusiastic stories about people he had talked to. Last week a couple from San Francisco had visited the store and they had given him their number in case he ever came to California. Remember, mom? Asma?'

The mother and the other sister remembered.

'We were happy for him,' the mother said, 'but of course we knew that he would never get to go there and if he would, the people would probably not even remember him.'

Kate nodded and encouraged them to continue.

'It's just ridiculous that Rachid has been arrested, ' the other sister, Asma, exclaimed. 'He has never been in trouble. He is just our sweet, little brother. Ali was always the one we had to keep an eye on.'

'Is Ali your other brother?' Kate asked.

'Yes.'
'He works in a hotel, I understood?'
'Yes,' the mother said. 'He is a cook. He has finally come around, but Asma is right. He was always a handful, with his quick temper. Rachid is the opposite. The youngest and truthfully the sweetest of all four.'
She looked apologetically at her daughters, but they just nodded and wiped their eyes.
Elias asked if they could show them where exactly the box with suspicious materials was found. Asma led them to Rachid's room and pointed to the bed.
'Underneath it. Surely someone planted it there.'
'How could they have come in?'
The sister walked to the window and opened it. It gave access to a roof terrace. From their roof, the sister explained, it was easy to get to other roofs and eventually to the street. Someone could easily have put the box underneath Rachid's bed, she said and Kate had to admit that she could be right.

When they were back in the car Kate received a message from London with Fatima Nouri's number. She asked Elias to call her and introduce her. It was easier this way, she knew. A call from the DST would make the woman cooperative right away.
When Elias passed her the phone, she asked Ms. Nouri if she had taken a German tour group to the pharmacy in the morning of the attack.
'Yes, that's correct,' Fatima Nouri said.
'Did you see anything suspicious?'
'No, I have already wondered about that myself, but sorry, nothing.'
'Did anyone in the group mention anything later?'
'No.'

'Did people in the group talk about the attack?'
'I guess so, but I'm not sure. Our tour ended ten minutes after our visit to the pharmacy and I didn't see them anymore after that. I just talked to Helga over the phone in the evening. About the attack and how lucky we had been.'
'And Helga is…?'
'The tour leader of the German group.'
'Okay. That brings me to my last question, Ms. Nouri. Do you know where Helga and her group are now?'
'Yes. They're in Essaouira. Their tour ends with a few beach days there.'
'Do you know which hotel they are staying at?'
'At Le Médina on the boulevard.'
'Could you send me Helga's phone number?'
'Of course.'
'Thank you, Ms. Nouri.'
She ended the call and turned to Elias, who was patiently waiting for her to see where they were headed next.
'How far is Essaouira from here?'
'Essaouira?' her asked. 'About two and a half hours, I'd say. Why?'
'I need to go there,'
'When?'
'Today. Now.'
'Why?'
She took a deep breathe and told him about her hunch, about the possibility that one of the German tourists could have accidentally taken a picture or video with information that could help them further.
'It seems like a long shot,' Elias said. He pointed out that they probably had the perpetrator in custody already, but then he nodded and admitted that he liked

her way of thinking and yes, he understood where she was coming from. So if she didn't mind, he could take her to Essaouira. It was late already and if they had to look for a car and driver for her, she would only lose more time. What they could do, he suggested, was swing by her hotel and his apartment to pick up some clothes and be on their way. Kate did the math quickly. They could be there in three to four hours. Between seven and eight. She could call this Helga from the car and ask her to gather her group in the hotel tonight. In an ideal world they could be back here at midnight, but she knew some things might take longer than she would like. So yes, agent Ramzi's plan was all right. She began to like him too, she thought. Who knows, perhaps she would even allow him to call her Kate.

FIVE

The road from Marrakech to Essaouira was not very exciting. The landscape was flat and barren, the road a straight line heading west. They passed through dusty villages where women seemed to be doing all the work, while men sat in the shade, drinking coffee. Not good, Kate thought and she said so to Elias. He laughed at her bluntness and surprised her when he said that he agreed with her. He had lived in France, he told her, so perhaps that's why he saw things differently now. Besides, he added, he was a man from the city, where everything was more equal nowadays. Many women had good positions in education, big companies and even the police force.

'Are you marrried?' Kate asked.

'In Morocco every man my age is married.'

Kate looked at his handsome profile. The long eyelashes and strong chin. She estimated his age at about forty-five.

'Do you have children?'

'Three. Two boys, one girl. And you?'

She shook her head, then added that, yes, she was married.

'Is that hard to combine with your travels?'

'Who says I travel a lot?'

He shrugged and said he assumed that, because she had been sent here too, hadn't she? It was her turn to smile

now and she explained that she traveled a lot indeed, but that she and her husband were okay with it. He asked her then where she had been before Morocco and they talked about that for a while. Zimbabwe, African politics and the politics of other countries.
In a small town called Sidi Mokhtar they stopped for gas and a quick coffee. After this stop the landscape changed and became prettier. Green hills with strange looking trees she had never seen before.

'Arganias,' Elias explained. 'The trees they get the argan oil from. Wait until you see the goats.'

'Goats?'

'Wait.'

Ten minutes later they passed them. Goats up in the trees like statues, with shepherds waving at the passing cars.

'What the hell?' Kate asked.

'Goats eat the nuts, so they do climb those trees sometimes. However, it's become a tourist attraction so these shepherds put them in the trees along the road in the hope that people stop for a picture and a tip. They're always in these same trees. You see that one of the trees is not even alive anymore?'

A few kilometers before they reached Essaouira the road began to climb and eventually gave them a good view of the Atlantic Ocean and the town below. As they drove down Elias pointed out the Île de Mogador, the island that almost blocked the entrance to the bay.

'Neither the mosque nor the prison on the island are in use anymore. The only people who go there nowadays are birdwatchers.'

Kate took it all in, this great view of a town that she heard about from a friend, who had been here and liked it a lot. She pointed at the coastline and the beach.

'Are those kitesurfers?'
'Yes, this is Morocco's windy city,' Elias said. 'Surfers from all over the world come here.'
They were on the boulevard then, driving past beach restaurants on their left and the old town up ahead in the distance.
'Did you watch Game of Thrones?'
'I did.'
'It was filmed here, at least some scenes were.'
'Really? Which scenes?'
'When that blonde queen, Daenarys something, liberated slaves, remember that? That was filmed on the ramparts and another scene, an assassination attempt, was shot in the port. I'll show you later.'
Daenerys Targaryen, Kate thought. Her favorite character of the series. Should she tell Elias that she had a slave too, but unlike Daenerys, had no intention to liberate him? See how he reacted, this liberal Moroccan.

Le Médina, the hotel of the German group, was a fivestar hotel on the boulevard. In the lobby they were greeted by a pretty woman with long blonde hair and a tanned face. Helga, the German tourleader, who apologized right away. Her group was free these days and she hadn't been able to reach all of her clients yet. Some had gone out for dinner in the medina probably and others hadn't returned to the hotel yet. Kate had been afraid of that, but suggested that they start with the people who were here. The hotel let them use a conference room and ten minutes later the interviews commenced. Helga stayed at Kate's side to translate when necessary. There were two things Kate asked the Germans: Did you see anything suspicious in or outside the Berber pharmacy? And did you take photos? They

talked to more than twenty people. They came in couples, most of them were around sixty or older. Similar faces, similar clothes. Serious people too, not just because of what had happened, but in general. At least, that was Kate's impression.
Two hours later they were still none the wiser. No one had noticed anything strange and although they looked at more than fifty photos, nothing of interest had caught their attention. When they called it a day there were just two couples left that they hadn't talked to yet. Helga promised to let them know when she got hold of these people, but that wouldn't be before tomorrow most likely.

Le Médina was fully booked, so Kate and Elias ended up with two adjacent rooms in Hotel des Îles, further up the road. They were tired from the drive and the interviews, but were not ready to go to sleep yet, so they went for a walk in the old town of Essaouira. Through the gate, past picturesque squares and blue and white houses. Elias told her about the town's history of slave trade and of the Portuguese, who had left their mark here. They walked up the ramparts and looked out over the dark and wild ocean. It would have been nice to be here with Roger, she thought, but the Moroccan agent was good company too. They had grown closer today. They worked together well and the roadtrip had made them bond.
'How about a nightcap, Kate?' he asked.
See? He was calling her Kate now and she didn't mind. He took her to a place called Taros, a rooftop bar with views of the town and ramparts. A band was playing, but not too loud, so it was all quite enjoyable. The waiter asked Elias if 'his wife' would like to have a

blanket and neither of them corrected him. They just smiled at each other and then she knew for sure that they were flirting. Both of them married, but not caring about that too much. She put the blanket over her shoulders. It was chilly here, much colder than in Marrakech and she had only brought a light denim jacket. They talked about the case some more. Elias didn't expect anything from the Germans anymore. It was a good try though, he said. Kate hadn't given up yet. Two more couples tomorrow, so you never knew. Elias talked about his marriage too. Although he didn't say it out loud he was clearly not happy with his wife. Or perhaps it was just his play whenever he fancied another woman. That he fancied her was quite clear now. That moment of complicity when the waiter called her 'his wife' had broken the ice and now he stepped up the flirtation. Light jokes were interspersed with the kind of sensitivity that he probably thought Western women liked. He casually touched her knee at some point and then let his hand rest there. It was all very transparent of course, but she allowed it.

When they were walking back to the hotel, he gave her his leather jacket which kept her warm. In the hallway, before going into their separate rooms, she gave it back to him and that's when he made the move she had been expecting. A bit clumsily he grabbed her around the waist and pressed his lips on hers. His hands moved up her back while he went for a real French kiss, probing with his tongue. For a few seconds, not more, she let him and even kissed him back a bit, but then she broke it off and stepped back.

'Time to go to sleep, agent Ramzi. Work tomorrow.'
She smiled at him though to show him that she wasn't rejecting him. She just didn't want to rush things, not

with a colleague. Besides, it had been a long day and she was tired.
Alone in her room she took a quick shower and brushed her teeth. When she looked at herself in the mirror she imagined the Moroccan's dark hands on her body. She saw him standing behind her, cupping her heavy breasts and playing with her nipples. The thought excited her and when she got into bed she first texted her husband to tell him that she had kissed with another man and then she masturbated and brought herself to a quick but powerful orgasm.

After breakfast Kate and Elias went back to Le Médina, where Helga was waiting for them with the two couples they hadn't talked to yet. They sat down with them and asked them what they remembered of their visit to the pharmacy. Nothing special, the Germans said.
'Did you take photos?' Kate asked.
One of the women nodded at her husband.
'Klaus takes hundreds of photos each day.'
'Could we take a look at them?'
Just like the night before they transferred the memory card of the camera to Kate's laptop and began to browse through the photos. She recognized Rahba Lakdima, where the spices and chameleons were sold. Then the narrow alleyway with the Berber pharmacy still standing. Photos of the group entering the building, a close-up of a fat man in a chair and there, at the back of the room, Rachid Mansour, the suspect, talking to a man. Kate felt a light, tingling sensation in her solar plexus. The man to whom Rachid was talking matched the description that he had given her yesterday. Perhaps he was just a good liar, but Kate didn't think so. Rachid looked frightened, as he was listening to the man. As if

he had just been given terrible news, for example about his family. She studied the man, but his back was turned to the camera, so other than that he was young, about twenty-five years old perhaps, and had short hair she couldn't make out much. It seemed to confirm Rachid's story though and that was something right there. She looked at the next photo, hoping to see the man's face from a different angle, but no such luck. Just more photos of German tourists seated in neat rows, waiting to learn more about medicinal herbs. It was at the end of the series though when they got lucky again. There were three photos in a row of the wife of Klaus, who was posing with a grin on her face and a small bag of Berber viagra in her hand. In the background was something that caught Kate's eye: an employee in a white lab coat who entered the room in the first picture. In the second photo she saw that he was carrying a sports bag in his hand and in the third he clearly put the bag underneath the table. There he was, she thought, the real perp. She looked at Elias, who also realized now that they had detained the wrong man. He took out his phone and called his office. In the meantime Kate copied the three photos and the one that might prove Rachid's innocence to her laptop. She thanked the Germans and when they had left she studied the photos some more. So we have two suspects now, she thought. One guy had come in from the street with the sole purpose to lure Rachid away and thereby framing him for what was about to happen. And another young man who would be easy to identify, because he seemed to have been an employee. Thrilled that her hunch had paid off she turned to Elias, who just finished his call. 'How did they react?'

He looked frustrated and said: 'My boss seemed reluctant. Not willing yet to let go of Rachid Mansour.'
'Why not?'
'Moroccan bureaucracy.'
'We should go back to Marrakech right away.'
He agreed and they went back to Hotel des Îles in a hurry to pick up their bags. Ten minutes later they were on the road. Both of them tense now, fully focused on the chase of new suspects. A case that had seemed a formality and just a matter of tying up some loose ends, was now wide open.

Halfway between Essaouira and Marrakech Elias got the message they had been waiting for. He had sent the photos of the new suspects to his colleagues at DST and they came back with an answer. The man who had lured Rachid away was still unknown, but the employee of the pharmacy, who had placed the bomb, was a certain Omar Bouazani. A team was on its way to arrest him, so more news would follow soon. Kate and Elias began to relax then. With a bit of luck all would be over by the time they arrived in Marrakech. They stopped for coffee at a restaurant where a man, who looked like Osama Bin Laden, served them. He had a long beard and was dressed in white. He seemed to disapprove of Kate, not looking at her when she asked him for the bill, but when they walked back to the car she could feel his gaze on her swaying hips and butt.

While still waiting for news on the arrest they picked up their conversation of last night. She asked him if he did that often, kissing foreign agents. It was the first time, he said, that he had kissed a colleague, but he admitted that he was not very faithful to his wife. He asked her the same, but she just said that she traveled a lot.
'Does your husband know?'

She shook her head, not wanting to go into that. Best to let him believe that he was her little secret. When she woke up this morning though and turned on her phone, messages of her perverted husband had poured in. With whom had she kissed? Was it just a kiss? And now what? Was she going to see this man again? She had answered him briefly, because her focus had been on the interview with the Germans. Now, as she let Elias talk about his time in France and the secret lover that he had there, she took a few candid photos of him and sent them to Roger. Just playing with him and driving him crazy while he was at work in the City.

SIX

They were having lunch near the trainstation of Marrakech when Elias got another call. The team had searched the building in which the suspect lived, but he hadn't been there. It looked like he had fled, because most of his belongings were gone too. A search warrant was sent to police all over the country and all they could do now was wait. Kate didn't have much patience though, not when they were this close. Remembering what Elias had said earlier on, that this was Morocco and here things moved slowly, she realized that there was one thing she could do and that was talk to Rachid Mansour again. She quickly explained to Elias why that was the best course of action they could take and he agreed. He made a few calls and miraculously enough they could go see the boy right away.

Rachid, they discovered, looked even worse than the day before. The skin around his eye had turned purple and his shoulders were slumped as if he had given up hope. He still denied everything, a guard told them and now they knew that he was speaking the truth. Kate pressed Elias to release the boy immediately and the Moroccan agent left the room to talk to his superiors. In the meantime Kate showed Rachid the four photos. The boy looked immensely relieved when he saw that his conversation with the stranger had been captured on camera. He realized that she believed in his innocence now. When she showed him the photos of the suspect placing the bomb he nodded vigorously. Yes yes, that was his colleague Omar.

'Tell me about him.'

'I don't know him well. He joined us two months ago.'

'Where does he live?'

'Near the airport, I think.'

That was correct, because Elias had heard the same from his colleagues.

'Is he from Marrakech originally?'

Rachid shook his head.

'He is from the south. From Rissani, I think.'

'Did he tell you that?'

'Yes.'

'So two months ago he moved to Marrakech to work in the pharmacy?'

'As far as I know.'

She thanked him and got up, reassuring the boy that he would be out soon.

'I'll ask my colleague to go and inform your family.'

'Where is Rissani?' she asked Elias.

They were standing on the pavement in front of the Mamouina hotel, about to go their own way for the rest of the afternoon.

'South of the High Atlas. It's more or less the closest town to the Sahara desert.'

'Do the police know that this Omar is from there originally?'

'I think so.'

It was an answer that annoyed her to no end and she told him so.

'Look, I understand that everything moves at a different pace here, but a team should be searching this entire town of Rissani as we speak. Your answer doesn't give me much confidence in the DST. As a matter of fact, I think we should go there ourselves.'

'Go to Rissani?' Elias asked incredulously. 'That's a lot further than Essaouira.'

'I don't care,' Kate said. She had placed her hands on her hips, looking bossy and quite intimidating. The Moroccan thought so too apparently, because he stammered and already began to plan the trip. If she really insisted, he said, they could leave tomorrow morning. Tonight, he reminded her, they were expected to attend a memorial service at the consulate. She nodded impatiently. He didn't need to tell her that. She hadn't forgotten. But okay, she agreed, leaving tomorrow morning would be fine if the Moroccan police hadn't arrested this Omar before. They split up then. Elias was going to Rachid Mansour's family to tell them that the boy would be released soon and Kate wanted to freshen up and get ready for her meeting with Ben Mitchell of the CIA.

They met in the garden of the hotel again. Ben Mitchell was more relaxed than a couple of days ago. Probably happy that other people had come in and taken over, she thought. He was still CIA though, so she brought him up to speed about the latest developments. In return he didn't have much to offer. No news from his side. His focus had already shifted back to the security of Cindy Stones and the president's son, who were expected in Marrakech in four days. Ben Mitchell explained that there had been talk about canceling the concerts or at least canceling the stay of the singer's famous lover, but to no avail.

'Wait,' Kate interrupted him. 'The president's son is accompanying Cindy Stones? You didn't tell me that the other day. I also didn't see anything about it in the paper.'

'It's top secret,' Ben Mitchell said. 'Not many people know about it, but yes, he is joining her and when my bosses tried to talk him out of it, he refused to even consider the risks. And well, he is probably right. The damage is already done and he has promised to stay under the radar. No walks in the medina for them, no Djemaa el-Fna. They'll be in a secure luxury hotel on the outskirts of town and they'll stay there most of the time. I'll be glad when their visit is over though.'

He sighed and added: 'To tell you the truth, we'd be even happier if they split up. Someone that close to the president marrying a pop artist like Miss Stones is not what the agency needs.'

In a café in the northern part of the old medina a man, who sometimes wore a burgundy djellaba, was drinking tea with his friend. They had met in Mecca, many years ago. Millions of muslims from all over the world and they had run into each other, two men who were born and raised in the same city in Morocco. They had an immediate click too. The same view on religion and the dangers that threatened it. The Big Satan, they agreed, was America, together with Israel and its European allies and everything was allowed to stop them corrupt the world any further. Gay marriage, abortion, the way their women behaved, it was all disgusting and perverted in their eyes. Then the so called war on terror started, oppressing the Arabic brothers even more. All to the advantage of Israel of course, because wasn't it the Jewish lobby in America that made the big decisions in the background? In those years both men were not yet where they were now career wise, but they had bonded and their friendship never faltered. Whatever happened, they knew they could count on each other. Now the one who was a bit older than the other, was asking questions. The other answered them as well as he could. Then they discussed the possible dangers and how to proceed.

'We did well,' the older man said. 'Everything is still going according to plan. All we need to do is stay calm and soon it will all be over.'

The man, who sometimes wore the burgundy djellaba, drank his tea and nodded, not wanting to show his friend that he was worried.

After meeting with Ben Mitchell Kate retreated to her room. She made some calls to London, mostly to get them to put pressure on the DST. She also checked the map of Morocco to see where Rissani was located. Like Elias had told her it was in the southeast corner of the country, close to the Sahara and the Algerian border. She wondered if it was really a good idea to go there tomorrow. It looked like a long drive indeed and if it led to nothing they would waste a lot of time. On the other hand, waiting around Marrakech, depending on the local police force, was not an option either. She was here to follow her own line of investigation and if that led her further south, so be it.

Before going to the memorial service in the consulate she showered and got dressed. Where ever she went, one compartment of her suitcase always contained clothes for a formal or elegant occasion. She laid out her dress on the bed and unpacked a new pair of sheer pantyhose. She sat down, slipped a foot in the black

nylon and slowly pulled up the fabric over her shapely legs. No stockings tonight of course, not to a memorial service. She walked over to the mirror and plugged in the blow dryer. While she dried her hair she looked at her body and remembered something Roger had told her the other day when she came out of the shower.
'Your body, my dear Kate, is almost daunting.'
'Explain yourself, slave,' she had said and they laughed at that.
'What is there to explain? Look at yourself, look at those curves. They intimidate the hell out of me sometimes. Such a woman!'
She was used to her own body of course, but when she was being honest she knew that her breasts were bigger, her hips wider, her waist narrower and her butt rounder than most women's.
'A perfect hourglass body,' Roger would say.
She imagined him sitting on the bed now, looking up at her. That was something else he raved about, her height. Five feet eight, as tall as he was, until they went out or played in their dungeon and she put on heels. Then she was taller than he was and he absolutely loved that! His daunting mistress, he sometimes called her. What would Elias think of her if he would see her like this in her black, lacy bra and the matching panties visible underneath her tights. She put the blow dryer down and stepped into her dress. Christian Dior, a gift from Roger. Expensive, but gorgeous. It subtly highlighted the very curves that he liked to rave about. It came to her knees and was much more modest than the sexy dress she had worn the other night in London. A different occasion of course. Last she took her heels from the suitcase. Black Louboutins that she had bought in Paris last year. Four inch heels and incredibly

elegant. She loved them and had worn them on several formal occasions already. Before she left she combed her thick, black hair and applied lipstick and eyeliner. A last check of her purse to see if she had her phone, make-up and an extra pair of tights and then she was all set.

The memorial service was as serious, subdued and formal as she had expected. The British ambassador gave a speech and there was a moment of silence afterwards. Condolences were then expressed to family members of the victims who had come over. Afterwards people mingled. Moroccan politicians, foreign diplomats and investigators discussed the terror attack and the implications it would have on the local economy and politics. Meanwhile the unfortunate souls who had lost their loved ones consoled one another. Kate talked to the British ambassador's wife Eileen, who asked about her father and who had apparently known her mother too.
'You look just like her,' Eileen said, 'but if you don't mind me saying it, you are even more beautiful than she was.'
Kate accepted the compliment gracefully and steered the conversation back to the present, asking Eileen about the big shots in the room. Who was that man over there? A government official? And that one, was he a general? Eileen, a blonde woman in her fifties, knew everything about everyone. Yes, she told Kate, that was general Azizi, a friend of the prime minister who was originally from Marrakech, Standing next to him, the woman with the glasses, that was Morocco's new minister of justice. Kate was impressed. Elias had told her that women in Morocco held some high

positions and now she was looking at one of them herself. She remembered the drive to Essaouira though, seeing all those poor women doing hard labour while their husbands sat around doing nothing. She was about to mention it to Eileen when her phone beeped. She took it out of her purse and saw that it was a message from Helga, the German tour leader.

It said: 'Dear Mrs. Davenport, this afternoon a man in my group remembered that he had not only taken photos with his camera, but also recorded a video with his phone. He showed you the photos this morning. The video I'm sending to you now. There is probably nothing of interest in it, but I wanted to make sure you are not missing anything. Best regards. Helga.'

A second later the video was downloaded to Kate's phone. She excused herself and went into the garden where she sat down on a bench in a quiet corner to watch the video. The German tourist, she saw, had started filming at the end of the visit to the pharmacy. There was a lot of yelling and laughter in German. Kate didn't get the jokes that were made, but got the feeling that she didn't miss much. The tourist went out through the door then, stepping into the alleyway. 'Also das ist eine Strasse in Marrakech,' he said to the camera. Showing a street in Marrakech, that much she did understand. He swung the camera to the left and focused on a fat man in a chair. The owner of the pharmacy. She had seen photos of him and people had mentioned his name. She had hoped to see more incriminating images of Omar Bouazani, the boy who had put the bomb underneath the table, but no such luck. Although the suspect had been in the same room as the German, the camera of the tourist had missed him. There was more laughter then, as the others came

out too and almost bumped into the American and
British tourists who were waiting to go in. The camera
danced up and down as the German walked into the
alley. It was then that she saw it. There, behind the
group of people who were about to be the victims of a
horrible attack. A man in a dark red djellaba, who was
looking at the entrance of the pharmacy. He was almost
hidden in the darkness of the narrow street. The video
remained unstable as the German kept walking. A
shoulder of someone blocked the image then. Kate
cursed, but didn't take her eyes of the screen. When the
road was clear again the video had almost reached its
end. Almost, because the very last thing she saw was
the man in the djellaba turning his head away from the
camera. She felt her heart beat faster. That man was
part of it. She felt it in her bones. She looked at the
video again and then a third time. She paused it and
played with the brightness. The problem was that the
resolution appeared to be low and the man had stood at
the end of the alley. Whatever she tried, she couldn't
see his face. Maybe they could do more in London, she
thought, so she forwarded the video to her contact at
MI6 and explained briefly what she needed. She looked
at the video again then and now focused on the man's
djellaba. Dark red, not a colour she had seen here very
often. Most men wore green, gray or black djellaba's.
And white of course. But dark red not so often.
Besides, now that she looked closely, the hem of the
hood was not red, but yellow. A small detail and good
luck finding the djellaba in a city of a million people,
but it was more than nothing. Damned, she thought,
why couldn't she see the man's face? Again she looked
at the video, in the hope to discover something else, but

the quality of the images stayed the same of course, so eventually she had to give up.

'What is a pretty woman like you sitting here by herself?' a voice asked.

She looked up and saw that general walking toward her. What was his name again? Azizi? Well, here he was, looking like a really smug authoritarian, with his gray mustache and ramrod posture. His dark eyes taking her in, her face, her breasts and her long legs. Not feeling self-conscious or shy about it. In contrary, with his hawkish nose and aggressive gaze he seemed to challenge her to do something about it. A man who was used to getting his way with women, no doubt.

'You're general Azizi.'

'How do you know?'

'Someone told me about you.'

'The ambassador's wife,' he said. 'Eileen.'

'You're very observant.'

'Only when it comes to beautiful women.'

'Don't try to flatter me, general.'

She got up and faced him. She was taller than him.

'Was there something else you wanted to ask me?'

'No,' he said. 'I came here to smoke a cigarette.'

'Good for you.' And with that she walked past him, back to the house.

'Mrs. Davenport,' he said, when she was about to open the door. She stopped in her tracks.

'Yes?'

'Be careful.'

'Excuse me?'

'You heard me,' he said. 'You might speak Arabic, but remember that this is Morocco. This place can be very dangerous for you.'

'Are you threatening me, general?'

'Not at all. Just looking out for you. Have a nice evening.'
He put a cigarette in his mouth and lit it. Inhaling deeply he walked to the back of the garden, pretending she wasn't there anymore.
Inside the consulate she bumped into Elias. She asked him if he knew general Azizi. He said, yes, he had met him, but didn't know him well. Why? What happened? And when she told him, he shook his head in disapproval. Perhaps, he suggested, they could go somewhere else, just the two of them.

The Renaissance Hotel was a fancy, artdeco hotel in Gueliz. From the roof terrace on the sixth floor one could see the lights of Avenue Mohammed V and the Koutoubia mosque in the distance. The agent of the DST had picked the right place, Kate thought. In most other bars and restaurants here in town she would have felt overdressed in her expensive dress, Louboutins and 10 denier pantyhose, but here she was okay. They found a comfortable sofa with a view and a sweet waitress brought them their drinks. Kate felt the tension slowly flow out of her body. They were just words probably, the threat of the machista general. Seeing that she was not receptive to his flattering, he had become aggressive. What had made her nervous too was that he knew her name, even though they had never met. But she knew his name as well, so perhaps someone had also just mentioned her to him. Elias agreed with that and told her not to worry about the general.
'He probably felt attracted to you, just like I do.'

Oh, how cheesy, she thought. But kind of sweet too, seeing the desire in this man's dark eyes as he almost stared at her curvaceous body.

'I've told my wife that I'm leaving for Rissani tonight.'

'That's quite an assumption you're making there, agent Ramzi.'

'I want you, Kate. I keep thinking about kissing you last night.'

She looked into those dark brown eyes and again noticed the extremely long eyelashes. She knew then that she would take him back to her room, but decided to let him dangle a bit longer first. She raised her glass and said: 'To a successful trip to the Grand Sud.'

He shook his head in frustration, but then asked her if she had read up on it.

'Yes. I know all about kasbahs and slavetrade now. I read it's beautiful down there. Have you ever been?'

'Of course,' he said. 'I was stationed in Ouarzazate for a few years.'

Then he looked at her again with that romantic longing. 'We can get a nice hotel there.'

She patted him on the knee and said: 'Calm down, agent Ramzi. I haven't even decided yet if you can stay with me tonight.'

'Why? You want it too and we both know it. Is it because of your husband?'

'No, my husband has nothing to do with it. I do whatever I feel like doing. I told you that.'

'So what's the problem then?'

'No problem, agent Ramzi. I'm just not in a hurry. She leaned back into the comfortable cushions of the sofa and crossed her long legs.

'So tell me about your time in Ouarzazate.'

He sighed, but then resigned himself to her pace. He told her about living in the south, about long and boring days in the heat and some of the assignments he worked on there.

Half an hour later, when he was at the counter paying the bill, Kate called Roger quickly.

'I don't have much time, my love. Just wanted to let you know that I'm taking the handsome agent back to my room.'

'Oh my god!' Roger exclaimed and before he could ask a million questions, she told him that she would call him tomorrow with more details.

In the brightly lit elevator Elias couldn't control himself any longer and tried to kiss her, but his clumsiness annoyed her so she pushed him away. He didn't get it though and tried again and that's when she slapped him. Harder than she intended to, but first that general had threatened her and now the agent, whom she did fancy, was all over her in a public space in a muslim country. So when the slap landed on Elias's cheek the sound echoed between the walls of the elevator. For a moment she thought he was going to hit her back, but he looked more shocked than angry.

'Look,' she said, 'you can come back with me to the Mamounia and spend the night. But until we're there, control yourself, okay?'

The Moroccan nodded obediently now, not wanting to risk his luck and be sent on his way after all. He behaved well during the taxi ride too and was a perfect gentleman when they arrived at her hotel, opening doors for her and letting her go first into the elevator. Kate didn't show a sign of anticipation either, but as they walked through the hallways of the hotel, she felt the excitement in her body. When they were finally alone in her room, everything happened quickly. They threw themselves at each other, kissing passionately. Her hands were in his hair and his in hers, then they were exploring each other's bodies. First while they were still dressed, a bit later with hands on bare skin and fingers fumbling and taking off clothes. His blue shirt and trousers, her dress and bra. His fingers on her nipples now, just how she had imagined it last night in Essaouira. His hand going down over her belly and underneath the pantyhose, to her big, round ass and then to the front, to her panties, softly squeezing her there. She reached out and slipped a hand into his underwear. His circumsized cock was on its way to being hard and already it was huge. She grabbed it and felt it grow in her hand. In seconds it became rock hard. She couldn't believe her luck, because it was one of the biggest cocks she had had in a long time. It wasn't just the length of about nine inches, it was also a really thick cock. God, just how she liked them best. She pulled down his underwear further while he kicked off his shoes and then took off his socks too. She looked at him briefly, at his handsome face, muscular body and the huge penis standing up straight for her. She stepped out of her Louboutins and took off the sheer tights and panties. They looked at each other for another second and then went at it again. They fell on the bed, kissing, touching, limbs entwined. She grabbed his cock again and jerked at it, but then he slid down between her legs and began to kiss and lick her wet cunt. The pleasure was from out of this world. Every time his tongue touched her swollen clit she moaned louder. She spread her legs as wide as she could and pushed his head deeper between her thighs. She got this close to having a monster orgasm, when he stopped what he was doing. He slid up over her body until they were face to face. She could feel his muscular body on top of her, touched his arms and shoulders and kissed him on the lips. Between her legs she felt his enormous cock pressing against her cunt. God, she was so ready for it!

'Come on,' she whispered. And then louder: 'Come on!' With that he slid into her pussy. She moaned with pleasure and he did too. Very briefly an image of her husband flashed through her mind. How he would have loved to see this, his wife fucking with another man. A man who had a cock so big that, god, she could almost feel it in her belly. Her thoughts of Roger disappeared then. All that remained was pleasure and pure lust. The strong body of her lover and the hard dick that filled her up completely, stretched her to the max and kept sliding in and out of her until it was just too much and she let herself go and came harder than she had come in years.

SEVEN

They left Marrakech early in the morning and headed south to Ouarzazate, a city on the other side of the High Atlas Mountains. The landscape was different from the flat and dry lands between Marrakech and Essaouira. This part of Morocco was much greener and fertile. Farmers worked their lands, often still with donkeys and thousands of poppies grew in the high grass on the side of the road.
Elias steered the Toyota Landcruiser with one hand, passing trucks and other cars like a real Mister Cool. The grin on his face said it all. Kate too felt giddy. Tired and sore as well, but in a good way. As the road started to climb and the views became more and more spectacular she thought back to last night. How many hours had they slept? Three? Or less? How many times had they fucked? How many times had she come? God, she had no idea.
Her phone beeped and it wasn't for the first time this morning. Someone in London was extremely excited, especially after she had sent him a picture just before they left. When they had woken up they had done it again. She had been on top and had ridden him until they both came loudly. She had collapsed on his chest, while he shot his semen deep inside her. Afterwards Elias had taken a shower and that's when she had taken the photo for Roger. A photo of her trimmed cunt with

the Moroccan's sperm leaking out of it, in places
sticking to her black pubic hair. Totally perverted of
course, but well, they both got a kick out of it, so why
not? The photo had probably sent Roger into subspace
right away. He sent her some voice-messages that
consisted of just weird sounds. She told him not to
masturbate, but suspected that he wouldn't be able to
control himself. A pity that she had to leave London in
such a hurry. This would have been a great opportunity
for her husband to be in chastity. But well, there would
be other lovers later, she didn't worry about that.
'This mountain pass is called Tichka,' Elias said.
'They're building a tunnel now, because many accidents
have happened here. Some years ago a bus missed a
curve and more than fifty people died.'
'Perhaps you should hold the wheel with both hands.'
'Don't worry, I'm a good driver.'
Kate sighed. All men were idiots, weren't they? But this
one at least had a perfect cock. She looked at him and
realized that she did like Elias.
'When you were stationed in Ouarzazate, did you go up
and down to Marrakech a lot?'
'Yes, I drove this road too many times, but it's
beautiful, right?'
She nodded and looked out the window. It was more
than just beautiful, it was magical. The mountains had
colors that she had never seen before. Red, green and
brown, but in different shades. And further up there,
there was still snow, while they passed palmtrees and
flowers down here in the lower valleys. In a riverbed
women were washing clothes and carpets. The ones
that were done were laid out to dry on the rocks.
Higher up, on the summit where a sign said they were
at an altitude of more than 2200 meters, they stopped

to stretch their legs. On the way down the landscape became even more dramatic with its red earth and old kasbahs that were made out of clay. A few miles before Ouarzazate Elias took a left turn and said: 'Let's take a little detour here.'

She wanted to protest and say this wasn't a vacation, but he insisted and said it would take no more than fifteen minutes and she simply had to see this. 'This' was Aït Benhaddou, the grandest kasbah in Morocco. Built up against a hill it was really more than just an old castle. It was an entire village, that consisted of clay walls and towers. She had read about it yesterday and therefore also knew that many famous movies were filmed here. They stopped at a viewpoint to take it all in. The dry riverbed and the barren red earth told her that they were getting closer to the desert now. It felt exotic and thrilling. She imagined the travelers from Timbuktu arriving here each month with thousands of camels that carried spices and gold, while the slaves had to walk. More than sixty days from Timbuktu to Marrakech. When they got to Aït Benhaddou, they had already made it through the Sahara, but still had the High Atlas ahead of them.

They got back in the car and continued. Back to the main road that led to Ouarzazate, where they stopped for a quick lunch. Then east, over a long and straight road, passing through towns with exotic names like Skoura, Kalaat M'Gouna and Boumalne du Dades. This was the famous Route of the Thousand Kasbahs, Elias explained. Although there were probably not that many, Kate saw kasbahs everywhere she looked. Sometimes restored and turned into hotels, often also in ruins. In Tinghir they got out of the car again to stretch their legs and because Elias wanted her to see the kasbah and the

beautiful oasis. It was a spectacular sight. The red rocks of the High Atlas and the lush, green valley.
'They're mostly dade palms,' Elias said. 'But the villagers grow all kinds of fruit and vegetables in their gardens.'
'The oasis is divided into gardens?'
'Yes, every family has got a piece of land.'
'How do you know these things?'
'My wife is from here.'
'Really? You're full of surprises, agent Ramzi.'
Kate walked to the edge of the rock. A soft breeze was playing with her hair. She was glad that she had chosen to wear linen trousers, because it was much warmer here than in Marrakech.
'Look, lady,' a little boy dressed like a Tuareg said, as he showed her a blue scarf. 'I give you good price.'
She shook her head, but told him that she loved his outfit, which made the boy smile.
'Let's continue,' she said to Elias.
They drove further east. In a town called Tinejdad they had to go slowly because hundreds of children on bicycles filled the road. Where did they suddenly come from, Kate wondered. After Tinejdad the road led through another oasis. Narrow canals separated the gardens, she saw now. Some of them were blocked on purpose, causing some gardens to overflow so the earth became fertile for the next crop. Up close the oasis seemed a little piece of paradise with birds, fruit trees, almonds and figs.
They came to Erfoud then, already close to the Algerian border. People still rode horses and carriages here and most women wore black burkas. Kate had read that the Moroccan government was trying to ban them, but that

news hadn't made it yet to this faraway corner of the country.

The town of Rissani lay fifteen kilometers south of Erfoud. The founder of the current dynasty of Morocco was born here, Kate had read. His son Moulay Ismail, who was also born in Rissani, became a very cruel ruler of the country. He had a powerful army of black soldiers from Sudan and was known to have fivehundred concubines and more than a thousand children. A man, in short, who might not have understood a woman like Kate.
Coming closer to the family home of Omar Bouazani, the suspect of the bomb attack, Kate had expected to see a lot of police activity, but all she saw were donkeys and people in djellabas. Were the police not searching the town? She asked Elias, who said that the DST and the police weren't exactly on good terms with each other. In this case in particular the police seemed to withhold information, he said. Kate sighed in exasperation. All the better, she said, that they had come here, right? Elias agreed with her. Good, because back in Marrakech he had thought her idea was ludicrous.
They parked the car on the edge of town and continued on foot. Soon they were in the ksar of Rissani, the old fortified part of town, where streets were narrow. Children followed them and Elias asked them for the house of the Bouazani family. People were much darker here than further up north, Kate noticed. When they walked on Elias explained to her that the ancestors of the people in this part of the country had come from across the Sahara, from countries like Sudan, Mauritania

and Mali. Descendants of slaves and the infamous black army of Moulay Ismail.

Looking for the right address proved harder than expected. The children had pointed them in this direction, an older woman told them to turn around and turn right instead. A man on a donkey showed them the right house at last. He even yelled the name of his neighbor, who opened an upstairs window and asked how he could help them.

'Are you mister Bouazani?' Elias asked him.

The man nodded.

'We work for the DST. We're looking for your son Omar.'

'Why? What has he done?'

'When was the last time you saw him, sir?'

'About two months ago, I think. He went to Marrakech to work.'

'Do you mind if we come in?'

The man, who probably knew of the reputation of Moroccan's secret service, hurried down and opened the door for them. The house was quiet. The man took them through a room with a tv to a kitchen at the back. A woman who had been cutting vegetables looked at them suspiciously.

'Police,' the man said to his wife. 'They are looking for Omar.'

The woman shook her head. She too was dark, like many of her neighbors. The father though looked like he had come from up north. Omar, she thought as she remembered the German's video, resembled his father more than his mother.

Kate and Elias sat down at the kitchen table. Omar's father poured them a mint tea.

'Has the police not been here yet?' Kate asked.

'No,' the man said and then asked them what he had been dreading from the moment he had seen them. What did his son do?

Elias told them and when both of the parents went in denial, he showed them the photos. Next, the mother started to cry, while the father cursed and pulled his hair in shame. Kate observed them and the shock they were in seemed genuine to her. One could never be sure though. Had Elias himself not told her that Moroccans were excellent liars? Was Omar hiding here? As much as she hated to mistrust grieving parents, she needed to make sure that they weren't being played like fools. She got up and asked the father if he would mind showing her the rest of the house. He looked puzzled for a second, but then understood and resigned himself to cooperating with them. Kate followed him upstairs, where the bedrooms of the children were. In one of them a little girl was playing with dolls, the others were empty. The man even opened closets and the door to the bathroom to show her that Omar was not here. Back in the kitchen Elias shook his head at her. He had come to the same conclusion apparently. They had come here for nothing. When they were leaving Omar's parents begged them to please not hurt their boy when they arrested him. Kate felt bad for them, especially for the mother who was wailing now and didn't care much what the neighbors would think. The same man on the donkey passed through the alleyway again and looked at the crying mother with big eyes. Kate and Elias headed back to the main street and walked to the souk of Rissani. There they showed the people a photo of Omar. Most of them nodded their heads. They knew him of course. The Bouazani boy. But didn't he move to Marrakech? No one they spoke to had seen him recently. After an hour of asking around they decided to call it a day and go back to the car. Just before they got in though, Kate heard the sound of a donkey approaching and a voice calling her. It was the man they had seen before. The man who had passed by when Omar's parents asked them to please not hurt their son when they arrested him. He was older than she had thought initially. Dressed in white, with gray hair and a beard, he looked like a local schoolteacher. A retired schoolteacher, she should say. She held up her hand to Elias, telling him to wait. The old men asked them if they were looking for Omar. Kate nodded. Why? Did he know where he was? In turn the man asked her what Omar had done. Kate decided to risk it and tell him. When she was finished the man shook his head in disapproval and told her that he used to be a policeman. He had known Omar all his life, but now felt compelled to help his former colleagues. A cowardly attack like the one in Marrakech couldn't go unpunished, was his opinion.

'So how can you help us, sir?' Kate asked.

The man looked at her intently and then told her that Omar's best friend didn't live here in Rissani, but in Merzouga, a bit further south.

'His name is Ahmed Abdelnour and he is trouble. I bet you my donkey that Omar is hiding there.'

When Kate had looked on the map earlier today, it seemed to her that the road ended in Rissani. South was the Sahara, east was Algeria. Now it turned out that the N-13 actually continued for another fifty kilometer, where the tarmac ended in the village of Taouz. Just before Taouz was another village called Merzouga and that's where they were heading now.

The road was fairly new and almost always straight, so they could drive fast. Arriving in Rissani had already given her an end-of-the-world feeling, but she felt it even stronger here. In the far distance on her right was a mountain chain. On her left, also far away still, she saw golden sand dunes that seemed as high as mountains. Around them there was nothing, just the road ahead that cut through the flat and stony desert. The only signs of life were a few small tornadoes, that whipped up sand and dust, and some tumble weeds that were bouncing toward the mountains on the horizon. Although they were driving quite fast, cars and motorbikes overtook them regularly. Most of them were rally riders and when Kate remarked that all of them seemed women, Elias told her that they belonged to the Aïcha Rally, a yearly contest in the desert for women only.

They were getting closer to the golden sand dunes and the village that lay at their feet. That was Merzouga, Elias said, but for now Kate only had eyes for the dunes. They were a spectacular sight! The sun was already sinking and the way its light fell on those magical hills was just breathtaking.

'That is pure sand, isn't it?'

'It is,' Elias said, nodding his head.

The Sahara, she thought. The traders from Timbuktu crossed this vast desert too with their camels and slaves. More than fifty days it took them to get here. Fifty days of just sun, sand and blue skies. Was it still possible to do it now? No, Elias had told her the border with Algeria was closed. Besides, Mauritania was not safe at the moment. But what a trip it must have been in the old days!

When they reached Merzouga they left the main road and entered the village. A group of children blocked the road. On their way to play football, it seemed. Boys bouncing a ball, others kicking it, while girls followed them on their bicycles.

'So how shall we do this?' Elias asked. 'We don't have an address for this Ahmed Abdelnour.'

Kate had wondered about it too during the drive, but seeing the children now gave her an idea.

'Stop the car,' she said. Elias breaked and before he knew it she was out in the street talking to the children.

'Do you boys and girls know Ahmed Abdelnour?' she asked as she crouched down and smiled, not looking like a secret agent at all with her ponytail and friendly demeanor.

Some of the children just laughed and others yelled something, but not in a bad way. One little girl though said that she knew Ahmed.

'What's that, sweetheart?'

'He is my uncle's neighbor.'

'And where does your uncle live?'

The girl pointed at a group of houses at the end of the street.

'Which one is your uncle's house?'

'The one with the red truck parked in front of it,' the girl said.

'And Ahmed, where does he live?'

'To the right. The house with the palm tree.'

Kate thanked the girl and got back in the car. She told Elias to park at the side of the road.

'Do you have your gun with you?' she asked him.

'It's in the trunk. I'll get it.'

'What do you think? Is he there? What does your gut feeling tell you?'

'I think he might be. How about you?'
'Yes, he is there. I just worry that he might have spotted us already.'
'Let's go in then,' Elias said.
They got out of the car and walked toward the house. When Elias approached the front door, Kate said that she would go around the back. Before he could protest she disappeared out of sight. As she walked to the back of the house she could hear Elias knocking. Through a side window she could hear someone hushing someone else. She felt an adrenaline rush, because now she was certain they were on the right track. At the back of the house she waited for what was coming. The sun was about to set. On the horizon the desert looked like pure gold now. There were no people around, thank god. No one to interfere with them, no one about to get caught in the line of fire. It all depended on what the men inside the house were going to do. She heard Elias knocking again and then yelling 'Ahmed Abdelnour, open up. This is the DST. I have some questions for you.'
Kate cursed him, because now they might attract the attention of the villagers after all. She heard more sounds from inside the house. Footsteps and the front door opening. Elias saying something, probably identifying himself. Then a voice raised in panic and a gun shot. Damned! Did Elias shoot someone or did someone shoot him? Part of her wanted to go back to the front of the house and make sure that her colleague was okay, but her instinct told her to stay put. Elias was a professional and he'd had his gun out when he approached the door. Chances were that he was alright and that it was the other man, who had gone down. That man though was probably Ahmed Abdelnour, not

Omar Bouazani, the one they were looking for. If she was right, this was exactly the place she needed to be, because if she were Omar, she would be ready to flee through the back the moment the DST entered the house. She looked at the backdoor intently, expecting it to open any moment now. Because she was so focused on the door, she almost missed the movement at the window near the other corner of the house. It was only because she moved her head to get rid of a fly that she saw it. Omar Bouazani climbing out of the window. He saw her too though. Their eyes locked and for a split second time stood still. Then Omar set off and started to run. Barefoot on the dusty street, his white shirt hanging loose and flapping in the wind. Kate went after him immediately, not losing another second. She was in excellent shape because of her daily runs along the Thames, but god, the guy was fast! Besides, he knew the village better than she did of course. All she could do was keep him in her sight, which was also not as easy as it sounded, because he turned corners where ever he could. They ran past a shop and a guesthouse. A young tourist with blonde hair, who seemed very much out of place here, stared at them with wide eyes. Not believing what he was seeing, this Moroccan men being chased down the road by a gorgeous woman. A hundred meters past the guesthouse Omar jumped a fence and ran through a backyard, that was really not much more than a private piece of desert with a donkey tied to a pole. Kate flew over the fence too, gaining on him because her jump and landing were smoother than his. A lifetime of martial arts had made her as agile and flexible as a cat. But then Omar surprised her by running into the house. What the hell? Who lived here? Another friend? Or was it just a desperate move? In any case she didn't hesitate and ran into the house as well. An oil lamp was lit but still it was almost dark inside. She heard furniture falling in another room and a woman yelling. Then she was in the room too, which was a mess because Omar had thrown over a table and a chair in an attempt to slow her down. As she jumped again, this time over the furniture on the floor, she saw the lady of the house trying to slap Omar, who was on his way out though the front door. When the woman saw Kate she focused on her and stepped in her way. Getting around and past her caused Kate to lose precious seconds. Although she yelled that she was police, the woman grabbed her arm and hung on to it for dear life. When Kate had finally shaken herself loose and got out of the house she was just in time to see Omar push a man off his moped.

'Damned,' Kate muttered as she tried to get to him before he drove off. She was too late though. The moped pulled up slowly, but just fast enough to stay out of reach. She looked around. It was getting dark quickly now. There, coming towards her, was another moped. An older man who drove very slowly. She stopped him and said the magic word: 'Police!' Miraculously the man obeyed her and got off his moped. Kate jumped on it. When was the last time she had driven one of these? In Greece probably, with Roger. She pulled up and looked for Omar. He had gained a hundred meters now, but she could still see him. If he were smart enough to turn off the moped's lights she would be in trouble, but he was probably too nervous to even think about that. He took a right turn and she followed, focusing on the red tail light. Where was he going? There were even fewer houses here. To her left it was just darkness and to her right she could just make out the silhouettes of camels. Most of them laying in the sand, some still standing and eating from a shrub. They were approaching the sand dunes, she realized. The road too had changed. The asphalt was gone and the path they were on was getting sandier by the minute. Up ahead Omar seemed to have more and more trouble to keep going, as his tail light swung from left to right. You little prick, she thought, you're not getting away. Omar got stuck in the sand then. Within seconds she was close enough to make out the silhouette of both Omar and his moped, that he threw to the side. It lay there with the engine purring softly and the headlight shining on a heap of sand. Meanwhile Omar sprinted away, off into the sand dunes. Kate braked, jumped off her moped and then she was running too. The only light came from the moon and a million stars. Omar's silhouette disappeared and appeared again when he reached the top of another dune. The swishing sound of his footsteps in the sand was another thing that Kate focused on. Together with her own footsteps and breath it was the only sound that could be heard.

They ran further into the dunes, which were becoming higher and steeper. Her sneakers were filled with sand, so she quickly took them off and continued barefoot. It cost her a few seconds, but it paid off because soon after she started to get closer. Omar was getting tired. She could hear him panting now. The fool, running off like that, straight into the desert. What was he thinking? Nothing probably, just trying to get away. The panting became heavier and his footsteps too. Kate was still okay, adrenaline running through her body, her mind crystal clear and focused on the chase. A chase that ended when Omar couldn't go any further. She saw his silhouette on the top of a dune. Bent over, resting his hands on his knees. Got you now, she thought. He saw her too though and yelled something at her in Tamazight, his Berber language. Kate approached him slowly. He had the advantage of being at a higher point and although he was tired she knew she was dealing with a dangerous criminal. A young man who had proven to be quite fit too. As she began to climb the dune he reached underneath his shirt and pulled out a knife. Great, she thought, where was Elias with his gun? She listened for sounds behind her, hoping that he was on his way, but all she heard was the two of them breathing.

'Drop the knife, Omar,' she said in Arabic. For some reason that seemed to enrage him. Because she spoke his language? Because a woman was telling him what to do? He yelled again and swung the knife in her direction. She saw a glimmer of moonlight on its steel. 'I'm going to kill you,' he said in a lower voice now. No, you're not, Kate thought, but she didn't say it. There was no point anymore in talking to him. He needed to be neutralized and for that she needed all her attention bundled in one razor sharp focus. She took another step up and again he swung his knife at her, but still more to warn her off than to actually hurt her. They were too far apart for that. Another step and now he yelled at her, calling her a bitch. Kate watched him closely. He was right handed and looked strong with his wide shoulders and good balance. Add the knife and she knew she had a worthy opponent. He was very agitated though, which made him unpredictable but also gave her an advantage. Her martial art training had taught her to always stay calm, so she could locate her opponent's weakness. Omar's weakness, she registered, was that he was too wild. He had swung the knife at her several times already and every time the movement had been the same. Wild and using not just his arm but his whole upper body. The fact that he was higher up on the dune didn't need to be a disadvantage either. Seeing how it could play out and knowing what to do, she took the last step up. As expected he swung the knife again, but she was still below him so she dodged it easily. At the same time she took advantage of the fact that his wildness was putting him slightly off balance. Too much weight transfer from his right to left foot and his upper body tilting forward. She placed her shoulder in his belly and grabbed the wrist of the hand that was holding the knife. All it took then was a quick pull. It was a move that she didn't need much strength for, but it had a maximum effect. His own clumsiness gave Kate the momentum that she needed. He yelped and then flew over Kate's head down to the bottom of the sand dune.

Meanwhile his wrist got twisted at such an angle that he was forced to drop the knife, which had been Kate's first priority. Quickly she picked up the knife and threw it over her shoulder as far as she could. She didn't need it herself, she just want to make sure that he couldn't use it either. Now the roles were reversed. Omar got to his feet as Kate came down the dune. He called her a bitch again, but didn't seem so sure of himself anymore. Kate, in the meantime, was still fully focused on him. The knife was gone, now the guy himself needed to be eliminated. Without the knife and after his fall his anxiety had grown and his movements became even wilder. When Kate came too close he panicked and jumped her, yelling like a Berber warrior. He tried to hit her with his right fist, but she dodged him again while taking another step forward and hitting him hard under the chin with the palm of her hand. He went down like a sack of potatoes and now it was her turn to jump him. Although he was groggy he kept struggling. She had been right, he was a strong guy and it was far from easy to overpower him. He lashed out at her a few more times, hitting her in the ribs and on her shoulder. At some point he even tried to bite her, the little piece of shit. Kate in turn stayed calm and went at it almost methodically. Twisting his arm and using her powerful legs to stop him from wriggling and trying to get away. It didn't take long. In less than a minute she had him where she wanted him. On his belly in the sand, with his right hand pushed up all the way up his back. A simple hold that was used by law enforcement officers all over the world. A hold that was very effective on Omar too, because if Kate wanted to she could break his arm in a heartbeat.

'Give it up now, Omar,' she said. To make her point she pressed her knee in his ribs, causing the guy to scream in anger, pain and perhaps humiliation. He stopped struggling though. Probably exhausted, but possibly wanting to fool her into thinking that he was surrendering. Best be cautious, she thought. With her free hand she took the phone out of her pocket and saw to her surprise that she did have coverage here in the desert. She called Elias, who answered right away. She told him where they were more or less and then all she needed to do was wait. Omar wriggled a bit at times, but behaved himself when she applied more pressure on his arm.

It took Elias a quarter of an hour to find them. He was accompanied by two local policemen, who handcuffed Omar and walked him to their car.

'How are you?' Elias asked with a concerned look on his face, but she told him not to worry and asked him about Ahmed Abdelnour instead.

'He is dead,' Elias said. 'He pulled a knife on me, so I shot him. I had no other choice.'

When they got back to their car she felt suddenly exhausted. The police car, with Omar in the back, stopped alongside them. They were going to lock Omar up in a cell in the village. Elias told them that he would join them there after he had dropped Kate off at a hotel. She wanted to protest and tell him that she wanted to go with him, but she was too tired and really, what would be the point? The suspect of the terror attack was in custody and now Elias, the DST and the police force needed to decide what to do with him next.

'You did great, Kate,' Elias told her. 'Thanks to you we've got him.'

She knew that he didn't mean what just happened, but everything that had led up to today. Essaouira, the Germans and the interrogation of Rachid. So yes, she could rest now and she felt grateful for it.

Elias took her to the nearest hotel, a place called Kasbah Tombouctou. She would have been happy with just a bed, but couldn't believe her luck when the place turned out to be incredibly charming. The building was made of clay like the old kasbahs and her room was spacious with a big, comfortable bed. She took a shower and then changed into a long dress and sandals. Elias joined her in the restaurant, where they had dinner and quietly discussed the case. Omar Bouazani was in custody. Elias and the local police had talked to him briefly and when confronted with the incriminating photos, he had admitted that he put the bomb in the room. He denied having accomplices and the Moroccan police seemed willing to accept that. Elias said that he had shown him the photo of Rachid too, the one in which he was lured away by an unknown man. Omar said that he knew Rachid, but denied knowing anything about the other man. The local police, in the meantime, wanted to wrap things up. Omar Bouazani, they had decided, would be taken to Marrakech tomorrow. They could interrogate him there, if they wanted to. Kate was not convinced that the case was solved. They might have arrested the main suspect, but she seriously doubted that Omar Bouazani orchestrated the attack. Who was the man in burgundy djellaba for example? Who had framed Rachid? And why had general Azizi threatened her? Wrapping up the case just seemed too easy, but for now there was not much she could do. So instead of worrying about it she tried to relax, enjoy the meal and their night in this magical place.

After dinner they went for a stroll in the desert behind the hotel. They saw the Milky Way and more stars than Kate had ever seen before. A boy, who was guarding a group of camels, greeted them and tried to sell them fossils that he had wrapped up in a handkerchief. 'They find loads of them here,' Elias explained. Kate wasn't interested, not tonight. She was too tired from their very long day, which had ended with her chasing Omar. When they were back in the room she could tell that Elias was hoping for sex, but the moment she got under the sheet she fell in a deep sleep.

She woke up at sunrise. A rooster was crowing beneath their window. She took a cold shower to wake up and quietly left the room. The sand dunes, she saw now, were right behind the hotel. The morning sun made them look more orange than golden. She climbed a dune and walked a bit further over the ridge that had been sharpened by the wind. Within minutes she was surrounded by the orange dunes. The only other shade here was the deep black of the shadows on the western side of the slopes. She sat down on a spot from where she had a good view over the desert. Over there in the distance, she thought, where the sun was rising, that must be Algeria. A country she had never been to, but now felt curious about. To her right, just a few meters away, a beetle left traces in the sand. Running away from here most likely. In the distance she heard the whistling of birds. The desert contained more life than she had expected. Looking at the sunrise she let her thoughts unwind. Images of the case passed through her head. The fight with Omar, the knife swishing through the air and Elias who had shot and killed Omar's friend. Then thoughts about Elias, his longing for her and the hot night they spent in Marrakech. And Roger, dear Roger, working hard in London. Living in such a different world from hers now. Soon she'd be home with him though and then all this would also have disappeared from her life. But now she was still here, in this beautiful spot in the Sahara, where life moved on as if nothing dramatic had ever happened. She sat for a while like this, thinking, musing and just absorbing her surroundings.

When she got back to the room, Elias just came out of the shower. He seemed happy to see her and kissed her on the lips. She laid a hand on his muscular chest and with the other hand felt between his legs. Just playful at first, but when his long, dark cock started to grow, she felt the temperature in her own body rise as well. He took off her blouse and then her trousers. When they were both naked and on the bed, kissing and touching, his phone rang though. He cursed and excused himself. 'Someone in the DST,' he said. 'Probably about the case.'

He took the call and disappeared into the bathroom. Kate waited, still hot and hoping there was no emergency, so they could finish what they had started. She thought of Roger then and of a way to make him really happy. She took the phone out of her purse and activated the camera. She placed it on the ledge at the head of the bed and smiled at the lens. A minute later Elias was back. They started kissing and from there things heated up quickly. She took his enormous cock in her hand and didn't let go until he was as hard as a rock. Meanwhile he fingered her. Both moaning now they moved into a sixty-nine position, from where temperatures rose even higher. Laying on their sides, driving each other crazy with pleasure, Kate lifted up her thigh to give Elias better access to her cunt and Roger a better view. She placed her hand on Elias' head, knowing that Roger would appreciate seeing her wedding ring. Then she shifted her focus back on the Moroccan's cock. God, it was big and thick. She could hardly put her lips around its purple head. She licked its length and kept masturbating him until he seemed about to explode. Kate herself was extremely wet by now and started to come. Her moaning became louder and louder, reveling in the pleasure that the Moroccan's mouth gave her. When he also slid a finger in her cunt she reached a deep and intensely satisfying orgasm, coming on the agent's face with the camera filming it all. They lay like that for a while, Kate slowly coming back to earth, her hand all this time around the big cock, keeping him hard and ready, because she knew there was more to come. A minute later she was ready and sat on top of him. Facing the camera now, it was as if she were looking at Roger. A smile that was hardly visible played around her lips. Elias didn't notice, but she knew that Roger would. She lifted herself up and reached between her thighs, again showing her husband the wedding ring. She took the Moroccan's thick cock in her hand and pushed the swollen, purple head against her wet cunt. Looking straight at the camera, at her husband, she lowered herself on this stranger's cock. Slowly it slipped inside her. It was so thick that it almost hurt, but god, hurting in a good way of course. And it kept going in, deeper and deeper until it filled and stretched her cunt completely. Then, when she was ready, she began to ride him. Slowly at first, but faster when she got in a good rhythm. Grinding her pussy against him, feeling a sexual pleasure that Roger's cock had never given her. Again the Moroccan proved to be a good fuck. He was hard and able to keep going without coming too soon. Exactly how she liked it, free to ride herself to orgasm, again and again. At some point, she had no idea how much time had passed by then, she turned around and rode him reverse cowgirl style. A favorite of Roger, although he was hardly able to do it himself, as seeing her on top of him like that almost always made him come right away. He loved seeing her do it like this though. Well, my dear husband, she thought, take a good look now. She sat up, squatting on top of the Moroccan and bouncing up and down his massive cock until she reached another orgasm. It was after this orgasm that Elias felt like taking some initiative too. He turned her around and whispered: 'From behind. Doggy style.'

He positioned himself behind her and slid his cock inside her once again. Roger, she realized, would see them from the side now. He would like that too, she bet, but then she forgot about her husband again as the pleasure of the pounding cock in her cunt overtook her. She spurred the Moroccan on, telling him to give it to her, to fuck her with his massive penis. Very basic and primitive, but it drove the man crazy and he began to hammer her even harder. Both of them moaning and growling like wild animals. Her round butt in the air, her weight resting on one hand, while she fingered herself with the other. Eventually they came together, waves of pleasure washing over her, with Elias' cock growing even bigger inside her, just before he exploded and shot his cum deep inside her hot cunt. They collapsed on the bed then, both of them not able to speak for a while, just laying there panting like lions after a chase.

Later, when she had a moment alone, she sent the video to Roger. She didn't look at it first, so she had no idea what the quality of the recording was, but ten minutes later his messages came pouring in. It had driven him crazy, was the gist of it. He loved it and mentioned all the details that he liked in particular. Well, she was glad to have made him happy, but they were about to leave Merzouga, so she didn't have much time to talk to him.

Omar Bouazani was taken to Er Rachidia Airport by the police, from where he would be flown to Marrakech. Kate and Elias were driving back to the city and because they couldn't do much anyway, they took things slower than yesterday. They didn't take the road back to Rissani, but went straight to Erfoud instead, driving on a road that stayed close to the sand dunes and passed hotels and a mine, where most of the fossils came from. In Erfoud the women in the black burkas were back. Walking the dusty streets in groups of three or four, they were on their way to the market or just coming back from it, bags with vegetables in their hands. Kate tried to get a closer look at them, but when the women saw her they covered half of their face too with the black veil, leaving an opening that was just big enough for one eye to look out of. What must their life be like? Could it possibly be any different from hers? They didn't travel the world, didn't have a slave at home and didn't get to fuck strange men they way she did just an hour ago. Or did they? She had no idea and would probably never find out.

In Tinghir Elias asked her if she wanted to see the Todra Gorge. Why not, she said, so they drove up to where the oasis gave way to steep mountains. Up in the gorge three hundred meter high walls towered up above them.

'Where does the road lead from here?' she asked Elias.
'Into the High Atlas, to a town called Imilchil,' he said.
'And your wife's family live here in Tinghir?'
'They are originally from here, but almost everyone lives in Marrakech now. There are just some uncles left, I think.'
'You're not afraid that they see you with me?'
'No,' he said, 'why would I? What do they know?'
Well, if he didn't care, she wouldn't either. They had lunch in a restaurant in the gorge. Afterwards Kate walked through the stream with her shoes in her hand. Today, she reflected, was a lot less frantic than yesterday and that was good, because she had hardly stopped since she was here.

They continued west, back to Ouarzazate. It was late afternoon when they got there. To avoid driving across the High Atlas in the dark they took a room in a hotel near the main road. It had a garden and a big pool and they relaxed for a couple of hours before having dinner. At night they fucked again, not as wild as before, but it was good nevertheless.

EIGHT

The next morning they drove over the Tichka mountain pass back to Marrakech, leaving the Grand Sud, the Great South, behind them. They had been there just two and a half days and it was intense, but Kate had loved it too. The magical landscape, the colors, the kasbahs and the feeling of endless space around them. Marrakech seemed like the modern world after their days in the desert. Elias dropped her off at the Mamounia hotel. He was going home, he said, to see his wife and children. Kate went up to her room and called Roger. They chatted for a while about their day. He asked her about her trip and the case, but knew that she couldn't tell him much. They talked about her adventures with Elias for a while too, in a casual manner as if they were discussing the weather. They had become veterans in cuckolding by now.
After talking to Roger she called Ben Mitchell, who agreed to meet her on the roof terrace of Café de France at Jemaa el-Fna square. By the time she got there the daily circus of acrobats, musicians, monkeys and fortunetellers was coming to life again. Tourists crowded the roof terraces of the bars, but Café de France was quiet, because it didn't offer the best view of the square. She found Ben Mitchell in the back where they could talk in private. She told him about Merzouga and Omar Bouazani. Although he wasn't the

most dynamic CIA-agent she had met, it was good to talk to him and get his feedback.

'I would like you to find out all you can about general Azizi,' she said. 'I have a strange feeling about him.'
Ben Mitchell knew who the general was, but didn't know much more. He had also just met him at the memorial service. She asked him about Cindy Stones and her famous lover. They were arriving tomorrow, he said. He was about to go back to the Mandarin Oriental hotel to oversee the last preparations for a lunch by the pool, which was planned for the next day.

On her way to the Mamounia hotel Kate called the British ambassador, who was still in Marrakech. She asked him about general Azizi as well. The ambassador told her that he was a well known figure in Rabat. He had been in politics before, but had now retired from that. Why did she want to know, the ambassador asked. Wasn't the case solved now that the right suspect was in custody? Kate told him about her conversation with the general and the uneasy feeling that was still haunting her. The ambassador laughed and said that she was just as obsessive as her dad, but then hurried to say that he meant that in a good way.

The last call of the day was to MI6 in London to obtain more information on the general, but MI6 had been briefed by the DST. They had decided that she had done a great job, but now it was time for her to come home. They had even booked her a ticket back to London for tomorrow afternoon. It gave her an uneasy feeling, as if influential people here wanted her gone. MI6, as secretive as they often operated, couldn't risk a diplomatic row with Morocco either, so at some point they had to retreat. This was that moment, she felt and she didn't like it at all.

In a luxurious villa in the palmerai, the oasis of Marrakech, a blonde woman kneeled down between the legs of an older man. She unzipped his pants and began to caress the man's penis, that in spite of his age, became hard quickly. She had seen hundreds of cocks and this one was nothing special. The man attached to the cock was a man of influence though. People in the club where she worked had told her that. The woman, Natalia, was born in the Ucraine. She came to Morocco years ago, thinking a job on a golf course had been lined up for her, but promises were not kept and she ended up working as an escort in Agadir. It was the man, whose cock she was now taking out of his pants, who had saved her from there. He had rented a studio apartment in Gueliz for her and made her his kept woman. Normally he came over to her place three times a week, but this week his wife was in Paris, so he had sent a driver to pick her up and bring her to this magnificent house in the oasis.

As Natalia opened her mouth and began to suck his cock, the man's phone rang. He picked it up from the side table and answered. It was his friend from Mecca, as he usually called him. Not feeling threatened by Natalia, because she still didn't speak Arabic or Tamazight, the men discussed the latest developments of their plan. The friend from Mecca was still nervous, but the older man told him to relax. They were almost there. All he needed to do, he told his younger friend, was go see the ghulam again and play him.

Ghulam, Natalia thought as she kept sucking the older man's cock, meant boy or servant. She knew that word, but didn't understand anything else. Nor did she really care. While the man talked business, she just wanted him to come quickly, so she could go back to the pool.

The next morning, after breakfast, Kate went for a walk. It usually helped her think and as long as she was still here, she wasn't ready to give up on the case. She walked through a green area of town that was called L'Hivernage. Many hotels with big gardens, she saw. She crossed Avenue Mohammed VI and came to the train station. She had a coffee in a café opposite the building and looked at the chaotic traffic on the roundabout as she kept thinking. A bomb had a killed a group of tourists, but the right suspect was in custody now. Why frame Rachid though? Just so that the culprit, Omar, could get away with it or was there another reason? She believed so, but apparently she was the only one. Ben Mitchell had listened to her yesterday, but he clearly didn't share her doubts. Elias had just laughed and told her to relax and let it go.

Kate continued her walk through Gueliz. She passed the Renaissance hotel where she had been with Elias after the memorial service. She crossed Avenue Mohammed V and saw the Koutoubia mosque in the far distance. Walking further she realized she was close to the DST building in which Rachid had been held. She supposed he was free by now. It was after she had passed the building and was just thinking about visiting the nearby Jardin Majorelle, that she decided to make sure that the boy had indeed been released. She turned around and showed her ID to a guard at the door. The man didn't want to let her in at first, but after she had given him a piece of her mind he stepped aside. She passed the empty reception desk and turned a corner. At the end of the hallway two men were talking to each other. One of them had a thick moustache and looked like he had some authority. She showed him her ID too and said that she needed his help. The man seemed annoyed that she disturbed him, but when she told him who she worked for he extended his hand and asked her to follow him into his office. When they were seated she asked him if he could tell her when Rachid Mansour had been released. The man looked puzzled though. Did he not know who Rachid Mansour was? She explained herself better, but the man was shaking his head now.

'No,' he said, 'Mister Mansour is still in custody.'
Kate couldn't believe her ears. They were supposed to have released the boy four days ago! What was going on here? Moroccan bureaucracy? Knowing that what she said wouldn't have much effect on the people in this building, she got up and walked out. She took out her phone and called Elias to tell him how fucked up his organization was. He was just having lunch with his family he said, but he would make the necessary calls. Kate was furious. She had thought about visiting the Jardin Majorelle, but she was no longer in the mood for sightseeing. Something was not right here, not right at all. She went back to Avenue Mohammed V and from there walked in the direction of the Koutoubia mosque. This was the modern part of Marrakech, with the same shops and restaurants as in England. Zara, Mango, McDonalds, etc. The people who came here to shop and eat were more modern than the people she had seen in the old medina. Less headscarves, more high heels and sunglasses. It was quite a walk back to her hotel and all the time something was nagging in the back of her brain. What was she missing? Walking on the wide pavement of Mohammed V, in the shadow of

the orange trees, she kept working her brain, trying to see things from a different perspective. When she got to the hotel she felt desperate though. Her flight was leaving in three hours, Elias would be here soon to take her to the airport. So again, what did she not see? Was it something obvious or something so elaborate that she would never find out, no matter how much longer she stayed? Could she really leave Morocco feeling that she hadn't solved this case? Was MI6 right when they said that she had done enough?

When Elias texted her to say that he was on his way, she began to pack her suitcase. Ten minutes later he knocked on the door of her room. She opened it without looking and continued to the bathroom to get her things from there. Two minutes later, when she came out again, she saw to her surprise that the Moroccan agent was half undressed and in the process of taking off everything. He had a big smile on his face and said: 'Let's do it one more time before you leave, Kate.'

She looked at his muscular body and his underwear dropping to his ankles now. His cock was getting hard already. Seeing him like that woke her up. He was right, one more time and better do it right, so it would help her forget this puzzle that she wasn't able to solve. She took off her shirt and bra and let him kiss her big breasts. He took one of her nipples between his lips and his teeth, which never failed to excite her. She took hold of his enormous cock and began to masturbate him. They fell on the bed, all over each other once again. He entered her missionary style and they did it like that for a while, looking into each other's eyes. God, she was going to miss this, she realized. He was a nice man and where was she going to find a cock this great any time soon? It filled her up completely, it was that big. She spread her legs as wide as she could and then put them over his shoulders, allowing him to enter her cunt as deeply as possible. Then he turned her over on her hands and knees and began to fuck her doggy style. Oh, how she loved it! She felt his hand in her hair, pulling her head back, while his other hand grabbed her hip. She moaned and told him to fuck her harder, which was exactly what he did. His hips slamming against her ass, his massive cock making wet sounds in her cunt. It was when he let go of her hair and she lowered her head, that her eyes fell on the heap of clothes next to the bed. Her brain failed to register it right away. She was overtaken by lust and all she could think about was that she wanted to get fucked like this forever. Slowly the image worked its way into her thoughts though. His trousers on the floor, covering one of his shoes, but there, right next to the other shoe, lay a dark red djellaba. She looked again, wide awake now, with his hard cock still moving in and out of her wet vagina. The hood of the djellaba had a yellow hem, just like the man in the video was wearing. Suddenly, in a split second, she understood. It was as if realization after realization was cascading through her brain. He was the one who had been blocking Rachid's release. He had shot Omar's friend in Merzouga, possibly without a good reason. And something else had bothered her in the back of her mind. After she had neutralized Omar she had taken out her phone to call Elias and had been surprised that she had reception. He hadn't tried to call her though, which a part of her had registered as slightly off. If she had shot Ahmed and he had gone after Omar, she would have called him or looked for him the moment he had been out of sight.

He had done neither. He had just waited, probably in the hope that Omar would kill her. All these thoughts came within just seconds. When she was convinced that she was right in thinking that he was involved, she threw her body to the side, causing him to scream in pain, because his cock had still been inside her. In one movement she kicked him against the chest. He fell off the bed and yelled.

'What the fuck, Kate?'

'You're one of them, you bastard!'

He got to his feet and began to deny it, but then saw the look in her eyes and stopped. He took a step toward his clothes, his dick losing its hardness quickly now. Well, that was okay with her, because all her lust was gone too. He took another step toward his clothes. Did he want to get dressed or did have his gun there? When he came even closer she jumped off the bed and blocked his way. He shifted his focus to her then. In the car to Essaouira they had talked about martial arts. He had told her that he loved kickboxing and now she remembered that. The gun, if he had indeed brought it, was behind her. Could she get it before he got to her? She doubted it. She would have to bend over and look for it in his clothes. It would make her an ideal target for a kick. So forget about getting the gun for now, just make sure that he can't reach it either. Focus on him, this man who had deceived her all along. A man with whom she had shared her bed and now wanted to hurt her badly. She could see it in his eyes. Gone were the longing looks and the camaraderie. He looked at her coldly instead now, calculating his chances. He took a step forward and although he didn't carry a knife like Omar did, she realized that Elias was a more dangerous opponent. Better trained as an agent and with kickboxing skills on top of that. Kate stepped back, not because she was afraid, but because she wanted to see how he moved. As could be expected from a kickboxer, he came at her with a low kick aimed at her thighs. She quickly stepped back and his foot missed her. He followed up with a left handed punch though. It grazed the side of her head, but still it hurt like hell. She was forced to retreat further, as he tried to kick her again. Her foot touched the djellaba on the floor and she felt something heavy weighing it down. The gun, no doubt! He swung his left fist at her, but this time she blocked him with her right arm and kicked him in the side. Then she crouched and picked up the djellaba. As fast as she could she searched for the gun, while she kept her eyes on her opponent. Elias knew that he had no time to lose, so he jumped forward and grabbed her arm. Kate's hand found the gun, but as she tried to take it out of the pocket of the djellaba, Elias hit her again, this time on the temple. He followed up with a kick on her left arm and that made her drop the gun. It fell on the floor with a loud thud and next thing she knew they were both on the floor too, grappling and trying to get the gun. For one short and dreadful moment he got hold of it, but she grabbed his wrist and banged it on the marble tiles. He yelled out in pain and the gun slipped from his hand. Kate knew that this was her chance. Apart from the gun the danger came from his power and his kicks and punches. Now that they were on the floor grappling, they were on her turf. She had always loved karate and held a black belt in it, but she was even more skilled in judo and Brazilian jiu jitsu. She held on to his wrist and tried to twist it. At the same time she locked her thighs around one of his legs and drove her knee up into his balls, feeling his testicles and cock against her skin. It wasn't within the rules of her beloved sports, but who cared? Elias gasped in pain. He instinctively felt that he was getting in trouble now. Not only had he lost his advantage of earlier on, he also felt the danger of being too close to her, like a fly that is getting caught up in a spider's web. Kate in the meantime got a better grip on his hand. Normally this is where she would stop, but this man was so dangerous that she pressed on until she heard the index and middle fingers break. Elias screamed out in pain and Kate recognized the momentum. Other people might have hesitated, but Kate was trained and experienced and knew that now she needed to follow up and finish it. Like a snake she moved around the Moroccan until she was behind him and held his head between her thighs, while still holding on to the broken fingers. She locked her right foot in the knee cavity of her left leg, making a perfect figure four and applied a deadly pressure on his neck.

'So you've been playing me,' she said. 'Who else is with you? And what are you planning?'

She relaxed her thigh muscles a bit, giving him some air to breathe and talk to her.

'Fuck you,' was all he said. His face all red and not looking so distinguished anymore.

She applied more pressure and said: 'I can kill you like this, you realize that?'

He just moaned and when she pulled back his broken fingers too, he let out a muffled cry.

'So you and Omar. Who else?'

Again she relaxed her thigh muscles.

'I don't know what you're talking about.'

'You bastard! You've been blocking Rachid's release. Why?'

'Just let me go and I'll tell you.'
'Yeah, sure.'
Again she applied pressure with her thighs, while she twisted his broken fingers at the same time. The Moroccan screamed and squirmed, stamping on the floor with his bare feet. Kate was just thinking about how to continue, when she saw the gun in his free hand. He must have reached it with his foot and somehow he got hold of it. He raised it, but she was behind and above him, so he wouldn't be able to aim at her. Nevertheless it was an imminent danger and she reacted accordingly. With her strong thighs she applied even more pressure than before and didn't let go anymore. She ducked away too and just in time, because a shot went off. The bullet pierced the wall behind her though. He pulled off another shot but that too missed her. Then the pressure on his neck became too much and he began to lose consciousness. First he dropped the gun, then his limbs stopped squirming and finally his body lay motionless on the floor, his head between her legs with the mouth open and face contorted. Kate still didn't let go. She couldn't risk that he would get up again. She needed to finish this and that's what she did. As much as she hated it, she strangled Elias with her strong thighs. It took another minute perhaps and then she was certain that he was dead. She got up and picked up the djellaba. In one of the pockets she found a wallet. She opened it, because she wondered if Elias Ramzi was his real name. It was though. It said so on his ID at least. She found something else in the wallet too. An old photo, which was maybe taken twenty years ago in Mecca. Two men looked at the camera, Elias and general Azizi. Well well, Kate thought, and Elias had told her that he hardly knew the general. Here they

were together in Mecca though. Elias, the so called progressive Moroccan who had lived in France and told her stories about his modern life that he enjoyed so much. The general, who had threatened her, was part of this conspiracy too, that was clear to her now. What to do next? Find out where the general lived and go to his house? She would have to be fast though, because somebody was bound to have heard the gunshots. Quickly she got dressed while she hesitated what to do with Elias' body. Shove him under the bed? No, there was no point. Soon the police would be here anyway. Instead she picked up her phone and called MI6 in London. She told her contact what had happened and asked for the general's address. Hoping that MI6 would solve the mess here in the hotel, she opened the door and left the room, leaving her suitcase and belongings behind, but taking Elias' gun with her.

NINE

Out in the street she stopped a taxi and told the driver to take her to Bab Doukkala. While she was waiting for MI6 to give her the general's address, the only thing she could really do was go see Rachid Mansour's family. Somehow that boy was part of it, she knew. Apparently it was important that he was kept in custody, no matter that he was innocent. She didn't know why and she couldn't go to the DST building to ask the boy himself, not after she had killed one of their agents. However, she could go see his family and talk to them again. After the taxi had dropped her off in the medina she found the house and knocked on the door. One of Rachid's sisters opened it. Asma, she was called, if Kate remembered correctly. The young woman looked at her angrily and when Kate asked her if they could talk, she let her in, but didn't offer her a cup of tea like last time. Once they were seated Kate decided to jump right in with her questions.
'Asma,' she asked, 'was my colleague here a few days ago to tell you that your brother was going to be released?'
The woman looked at Kate with wide eyes. Truly surprised, Kate realized.
'He was here,' Asma said. 'But he told us that Rachid was guilty and was going to be extradited to America, where he might be executed.'

'What?'
'That's what the man said.'
'It's bullshit. A lie. Your brother is innocent and my colleague knew that when he came here.'
'But why…?'
The two women looked at each other, both puzzled and lost in their thoughts.
'So you felt angry with me?'
'Yes, you work for the Americans.'
'Technically I work for the British government, but that doesn't really matter now. Important is to find out why my colleague wanted you to believe that Rachid was not only guilty,' Kate said, 'but also that he was going to be tried in America. He specifically mentioned America?'
'Oh yes, now that I think about it, he really emphasized it.'
'How exactly?'
'He must have mentioned America maybe five times. And he said that Morocco couldn't do anything about it. He said that the DST and the police suspected that my brother was innocent, but that there was not much they could do to stop the Americans.'
So for some reason it had been important for Elias to let this family believe that the Americans were to blame for their brother's misery. Not just when he came here by himself, when he should have told them that the boy was innocent, but right from the beginning. Framing Rachid for the bomb attack had not just been a way for the real suspects to get away with it, but seemed a crucial step in something that was still going on. All along Kate had suspected there was more to this case than met the eye, so it didn't really surprise her.
'Tell me about your father,' she said to Asma. 'When did he die and how?'

The woman looked surprised but answered: 'He did in a car crash some years ago. Just a stupid accident.'
'Are your parents originally from Marrakech?'
'My father was. My mother is from a town in the Anti Atlas Mountains.'
'Where did your father work?'
'He was a waiter in a café in the medina.'
'And your mother, does she have a job?'
'No, she has always taken care of us. My brothers are the ones who support us now that our father can't do that anymore.'
'What was the name of your other brother again?'
'Ali.'
She nodded at a framed picture on the wall opposite the sofa. A surly looking young man looked back at her. Very different from his brother Rachid.
'So that's Ali?'
'Yes,' Asma said. 'It was taken last year when he got his job.'
'And where does Ali work? I think you mentioned a restaurant or a hotel, the last time we spoke?'
'Yes, he works as a cook in the kitchen of the Mandarin Oriental hotel.'
The Mandarin Oriental, Kate thought. Ben Mitchell had mentioned it, because that's where Cindy Stones and the president's son were staying.
'We are very proud of him,' Asma said, but Kate wasn't listening anymore. Leaving the Moroccan woman behind with lots of questions she ran out of the room and flew down the stairs. Out in the street she looked left and right for a taxi and saw one at the end of the street. An old, beige Mercedes with the driver leaning against it. As she approached him she yelled at him: 'The Mandarin Oriental hotel, now! Fast!'

The man jumped behind the wheel and started the car. It was a twenty minute drive to the Mandarin Oriental hotel, he said.

'Make it in ten and I double your money,' Kate said. The hotel was located on the other side of town, outside the historic medina. She told the driver to go faster, assuring him that she worked for the government and that all fines would be taken care off. Then she tried to call Ben Mitchell, but he didn't answer. Too busy probably. She called her contacts in MI6 and the CIA too, while the car drove at high speed past the Koutoubia mosque and the Jemaa el-Fna square. Then they were racing through the mellah, the former jewish quarter, past small shops and people on donkeys. She told her contact in MI6 what was going on, but the Americans didn't answer. Five o'clock in the morning there, she realized, and her contact in the CIA was just one woman. She tried Bob Delaney then, but he didn't answer either. Meanwhile the car sped passed the Jardin Agdal and the botanical gardens. The driver asked her what the hurry was, but she had no time for him. All she thought about was Ali Mansour, who was a cook in the Mandarin Oriental. A boy who had always been a handful. His family had told her that a few days ago. It was just a remark then, to point out that Rachid was the sweet one. Now she understood though. As crazy as it sounded, the bomb in the pharmacy was just a small part of a much bigger picture. Killing a group of tourists must have been a nice bonus, but the real target here was the son of the American president. General Azizi or Elias must have got wind of him tagging along with Cindy Stones and they had looked for a way to reach him. That's when Ali must have appeared on their radar. A boy with a temper, who had a brother that worked with tourists in a Berber pharmacy. So what if, they must have thought, they could kill two birds with one stone? Plant a bomb and kill a group of tourists and create a perfect set-up for the assassination of the son of the American president? Frame Rachid for the bomb attack, hold him in custody and threaten his family with a horror scenario in which the Americans were going to execute him. Wouldn't that enrage the brother with a temper, who happened to be in a unique position to get close to the president's son. The boy was a cook in the Mandarin Oriental, for god's sake, and would prepare three meals a day for his guests. Kate knew she was right. The only thing that worried her now was that she might have discovered the conspiracy too late. Had Cindy Stones and her lover not arrived this morning? And didn't Ben Mitchell say something about a late lunch that he needed to prepare the security of? Would he have thought of a cook possibly trying to poison the people he was supposed to protect. She doubted it. They were all focused on bombs and guns these days.

She tried to call Ben Mitchell again, but again no answer. He didn't even have his voicemail activated. It would be up to her, she realized, to locate Ali Mansour and keep him away from the famous couple.

They arrived at the Mandarin Oriental hotel. At the gate she identified herself to the guards, but when they hesitated she drew the gun that she had taken from Elias and pointed it at the driver.

'Drive. Come on, go!'

The poor man stepped on the gas and they flew past the guards. The hotel was at the end of the driveway. It looked like a palace, with the snowy mountaintops of the High Atlas in the background. The driver parked the Mercedes at the entrance of the main building. Kate was out before the car had come to a complete stop. She ran up the steps into the lobby. There was another guard, but he wasn't too alert and she was passed him before he understood what was happening. In the lobby she saw the first American agents. Being one of them in a way, she recognized them immediately. Their blue suits, the haircuts and the way they looked at their surroundings. She identified herself and explained what was happening. The agents, a man and a woman, were professionals and didn't bother to ask her for details or a further explanation. They understood the president's son was in danger and that was enough to activate them. They began to talk into their mouthpieces, telling their colleagues to protect the American couple and keep them away from any food and drinks that had been served by the hotelstaff. Kate in the meantime asked directions to the kitchen. She then ran past the pool to a building that stood to the side. The door was open and she saw the movement of people inside. Two women, one older, the other still quite young.

'Where can I find Ali Mansour?' she asked them as she walked into the kitchen.

Thankfully the older woman pointed to a young man who was chopping tomatoes. He didn't see her coming and only noticed her presence when his arm was grabbed and twisted on his back and his face pressed on to the chopping board.

'Ali Mansour,' Kate said, 'you are under arrest for conspiring to kill citizens of the United States of America.'

The boy, because that's what he really was, struggled but she held him in a tight grip. After a while he gave up and began to cry. Kate felt bad for him, but what could she do? Two agents came in, one of them the female agent to whom she had talked in the lobby. They handcuffed Ali and took him away. Ben Mitchell walked in too, accompanied by a Moroccan agent. She told them about the conspiracy and as she was still talking the Moroccan began to make phone calls. Kate understood what would happen next. The kitchen area would be sealed and searched. She was convinced they would find the poison somewhere, or else perhaps a gun or a bomb after all. The boy hadn't denied the allegations when she arrested him. He had started to cry instead, a sign that he had been under a lot of stress. Pressure that had been applied directly by Elias most likely. The scheming bastard had gone to the family's home to tell them about Rachid's ordeal, but she was sure that he had contacted Ali separately to influence him and prepare the assassination attempt with him. Well, Elias was dead now and Ali was under arrest. She didn't know if there were many others, like the man who had lured Rachid away from the pharmacy, but that she might never know. However, she did know who was the other big player in this conspiracy. The one who had probably planned all this together with Elias: General Azizi. She recalled his creepy warning in the garden of the consulate. Even before that though he had said something that made her dislike the man. What was it again? 'What is a pretty woman like you doing here by herself?' The macho prick. And right after that he threatened her. Thinking about him now made her blood boil.

She walked out of the kitchen, followed by Ben Mitchell. They passed the pool where the American pointed out a group of tourists on the other side of the water. Kate saw Cindy Stones and next to her the president's son. They seemed shaken up by the sudden activity of the secret agents, but at least they were safe. Kate and Ben Mitchell came to the reception area. She told him about general Azizi. She explained that there was a chance to get him, but they needed to act fast, because before long he would find out that his plan had failed. Being a general he would cover his ass within hours, and a lot sooner probably if word got out that she was going after him. To his credit Ben Mitchell didn't doubt anything she said. Instead he suggested that he go with her. He had a car parked to the side of the hotel.

'Okay,' Kate said. 'Go get it, while I make a call.'
First she called her contact in MI6 in London again. They still hadn't found the current address of the general, she was told. Kate, who had thought of another way of getting it, didn't waste more time. Quickly she explained to her contact what had happened in the Mandarin Oriental hotel, who was responsible and what she was planning to do next. Now someone else knew at least, in case things went wrong in the next hour. After her call to London she called the British ambassador and asked him for his wife Eileen. Fortunately they were at home and Eileen got on the phone almost right away.

'Eileen,' Kate said, 'I have a very important question for you. You told me that general Azizi is from Marrakech originally. Do you know if he has a house here and if so, do you know where it is? Perhaps you even have an address?'

Eileen, bless her heart, said that she did, because a few weeks ago the general had given a party which they had attended. She had to look it up, but got back on the phone a minute later and gave her the address just as Ben Mitchell pulled up the driveway of the Mandarin Oriental hotel.

The general's house was not far from the Mandarin Oriental hotel. It was a bit further south, close to the road to Ouarzazate. Following the GPS on her phone, they reached it within a quarter of an hour. They parked the car in front of the house.
'How do we do this?' Ben Mitchell asked.
Kate had wondered about that too. An option could be to split up, one ringing the doorbell, the other one going around the back, just like in Merzouga when they were after Omar. She had met the general though and she couldn't imagine him fleeing through the back like Omar had, especially not from two foreign agents. No, she thought, best approach him directly.
'Do you have a gun?' she asked Ben Mitchell. The American patted on his side and nodded.
'How about you?' he asked.
'Yes, the one I took from agent Ramzi.'
She took the Beretta from the pocket of her jacket and placed it casually behind her, underneath her belt.
'Okay, let's go then,' she said.
They got out of the car and walked up to the gate. Kate pressed the intercom and looked up at the camera that was mounted on the wall. A female voice asked them who they were. A housekeeper probably. Not a security guard, which was good. Kate told the woman her name and explained that she needed to see the general because of a matter that concerned national security.
'One moment please,' the woman said.
While they waited, they discussed what might happen next.

'At least she didn't say that he's not here,' Ben Mitchell said. 'Now let's hope that he will want to see us.'
'I bet he does. He is an arrogant bastard. I also bet we've piqued his curiosity.'
She was right, because a minute later the gate opened. They walked in and saw what Eileen had described: a short driveway and a lawn and further in the back the villa that was surrounded by a lush garden. A woman came out of the house and welcomed them. General Azizi, she said, was expecting them by the pool. They followed the housekeeper through the garden to a big pool and a wooden deck. The general was stretched out in one of the reclining chairs. He was wearing black swimming trunks. Small ones, Kate thought, like Italian men wore. His chest hair was as gray and abundant as the hair on his head. He lifted his black sunglasses and smiled at them.
'Agent Mitchell, what a pleasant surprise! And you brought the girl with the beautiful legs. What a pity she is not wearing a dress today.'
Trying to get her worked up right away. She bet that he knew perfectly well that she posed a bigger threat to him than Ben Mitchell.
'What can I do for you, agent Mitchell?'
The American hadn't expected this and began to stammer somewhat incoherently. Kate put a hand on his arm and stepped forward. She took the photo of Elias and the general from her pocket and held it up.
'Does this photo look familiar to you?'
'I can't see it from here. Come a bit closer, pretty lady.'
Kate walked over to him and threw the photo in his lap. He picked it up and examined it as if he saw it for the first time.

'Of course,' he said. 'Agent Ramzi and I in Mecca. That was taken a long time ago.'
'Have you talked to agent Ramzi recently?'
'Actually I did. He told me you're a great fuck, Mrs. Davenport.'
And then to Ben Mitchell: 'Did she tell you that she and agent Ramzi are fucking? And she is married too, you know. In Morocco we have a word for women like that.'
Trying hard not to let him get under her skin, Kate focused on the one thing he had said that really mattered. 'She and agent Ramzi are fucking...' Present tense, so he didn't know yet that his friend was dead. How about the developments in the Mandarin Oriental hotel? Had someone told him what had happened there? Or was he still waiting for news? He seemed relaxed, without a worry in the world, but that was for their benefit. His phone was within reach, on a side table, next to the paper and a glass of iced tea and she was sure that he was eagerly waiting for it to ring.
'So if there is nothing else I can do for you, why don't you relax and join me here. Swim, eat, relax.'
He gestured to the empty chairs like a generous king and then noticed something that made him smile. He said: 'There is Natalia. Have you met my friend Natalia? Come here, darling.'
A blonde woman, dressed in a red bikini, walked over to them and nodded politely. She sat down on the chair next to the general and leaned over to kiss him on the lips.
'These people are American and British agents, sweetheart. The woman was also my friend's fuckbuddy.'

Natalia looked embarrassed by the general's bluntness, but nothing he said was really meant for her ears anyway.

'My friend Elias,' the general continued, 'says that this agent has fantastic tits, but I believe yours are bigger, darling.'

Kate didn't doubt that. Natalia's breasts were enormous, most likely thanks to plastic surgery.

'General Azizi,' Kate said, 'in a minute someone will call and tell you that Ali Mansour was arrested in the Mandarin Oriental hotel. He attempted to kill the son of the American president. We have reason to believe that Ali Mansour is part of a bigger conspiracy that was led by you and agent Ramzi.'

The arrogant bastard just laughed and said: 'Prove it.'

'I don't need to prove it. That's the work of the intelligence agencies and the police. They'll find the proof, I promise you that. Phone records, places where you and agent Ramzi met, mosques that you frequented, websites that you visited. I just wanted to tell you in person that your game is up. Before sunset you'll be locked up.'

'Perhaps you should leave after all, agent Davenport. You're insulting me in my own home.'

'When was the last time you talked to agent Ramzi?'

'I don't know. A week ago?'

'Liar.'

'Another insult. Be careful now.'

But this was exactly what Kate was aiming for. Get him worked up, just like he was trying to get under her skin. With his macho temperament it would be easier for her, she knew.

'So you didn't talk to him today?'

'No, but I'll call him tomorrow if that makes you happy.'

'Good luck with that.'

'What is that supposed to mean?' he asked.

'Your friend won't answer,' she said.

Something started to dawn in his eyes. They hardened too.

'Are you telling me that he is under arrest too?'

'Like your friend Ali, you mean? No, agent Ramzi is not under arrest. He is dead, general Azizi. I killed him. Not with a gun, but with my bare hands, or maybe I should say, with my 'beautiful legs'. First I broke his fingers and then I strangled him.'

Ben Mitchell and Natalia gasped in shock, but the general didn't move. The news hit him the hardest though. Kate saw it in his eyes. Right at that moment they heard the sirens in the distance.

'Police,' Kate said. 'Coming for you, you pathetic little man.'

And that was it, the last straw. His hand reached out to the newspaper on the side table. Kate had counted on the possibility that he had a gun hidden underneath it and she was right. General Azizi was fast for his age. In a split second he brought up the gun, but Kate had already drawn hers and pulled the trigger before he could take aim. The bullet from the Beretta hit the general right between the eyes, breaking the sunglasses in a hundred pieces. The back of his head smashed into the chair's cushion. A perfect hole had appeared in his forehead and some blood started to trickle out of it. When the echo of the gunshot had faded away all Kate heard was Ben Mitchell's heavy breathing and the sirens coming closer. Natalia was holding her head with both hands and looked at her lover with eyes that were wide open in shock. She didn't scream or cry, just stared in disbelief. Kate walked over to her and put an arm around her shoulders.

'Come on, let's go inside.'

Gently she led the woman away, while Ben Mitchell went over to the main entrance to open the gate for the police cars which were almost there now.

TEN

A week later Kate and Roger were spending a few days in Essex. First they had visited Kate's dad in his beautiful home near Castle Hedingham and the next day they drove to Colchester, where Roger had booked them a night in a luxurious spa hotel. All afternoon they relaxed and spoiled themselves in the various treatment rooms. Sauna, massage, a lazy swim, a drink and a nap. After killing general Azizi Kate had been taken out of Morocco quickly with the help of Ben Mitchell and the CIA. She had gone to the MI6 headquarters in London, where she was debriefed. Ben Mitchell, in the meantime, had called her regularly to tell her what was happening in Marrakech. Most important of all was the discovery of cyanide in a bottle of wine that was about to be served to Cindy Stones and the president's son. The Moroccan police had also searched the houses of Elias Ramzi and general Azizi. Documents were found that had proven them to be much less liberal than they pretended to be. Phone records had turned up numerous conversations with people in Saudi Arabia, people that were well known extremists. Direct proof was still lacking, but nobody cared about that too much. Both of them were eliminated after they had tried to kill an agent who was investigating the terrorist attack on the Berber pharmacy, so in the eyes of everybody involved that was enough proof right there.

Now that the case was basically closed Kate had suddenly felt exhausted. The danger, the traveling, the sex with a man who turned out to be one of the terrorists, it was a lot to handle within a week. So when dear Roger suggested they book a night in a spa hotel she had been delighted.

That night they dressed up for dinner, both of them feeling relaxed after a long day of getting pampered. Roger put on gray trousers and a blazer, Kate a cream colored dress and red Jimmy Choo's with four inch heels. Today had been the first day she felt that Morocco was behind her. It had taken her a full week to wrap up the investigation and process everything that happened. She knew that it would take her a little longer to forget Elias Ramzi, whom she had liked, but eventually had to kill. Roger, bless his heart, hadn't asked her any questions about her affair in Marrakech yet, even though she knew that his curiosity was killing him. Now though, as he opened the door for her, his gaze fell on the seams of her nude colored nylon stockings and his eyes lit up. Heels and nylons, usually a sign that his wife was in the mood to play.
'Oh,' was all he said. Pleasantly surprised, for sure. She had got dressed in the bathroom on purpose, in order to not let him see the kind of underwear she was wearing. That was going to be her little treat for him later. A treat in the form of a white garter belt and fully fashioned nylons, something that never failed to tick the boxes of her fetichist husband. For now though she would just let him look at her seamed stockings and imagine the rest.

In the restaurant a sweet waitress accompanied them to a table in the back with a view to beautifully lit interior garden. Kate crossed her legs and sighed.
'What a lovely day, right?'
Roger nodded. He looked happy too.
'You're back now,' he said. 'Really back, I mean.'
'Yes, you're right. I needed today, Mister Winfield. Thank you.'
The waitress came back and they ordered a bottle of Château d'Issan.
'I hope this time you'll be home for a while,' Roger said.
'Don't worry, love. I already told my contacts to leave me alone for the next two weeks.'
'That's great. Let's hope they'll honor it.'
'I think they will.'
Wine was served and when the waitress had left Roger said: 'I understand you had a lover in Marrakech.'
His eyes lit up in mischief and anticipation.
'Oh yes,' Kate said. 'A bad man, but a great lover. You've seen the video.'
'Tell me more.'
'What's there to tell, you little pervert? What would you like to know?'
Her eyes smiled too. She loved playing these games as much as her husband, if not more.
'I would like to hear all the details.'
'I know you do, Roger. Tell you what. Let's enjoy our dinner first. Later, when we're back in the room, I'll tell you all about fucking with Elias. How does that sound?'
Roger's eyes twinkled, but she could also see the lust looming in the back. Yes, they could play tonight. Perhaps she would even tie him up or give him a good spanking. Look for a reason first, but during dinner she had plenty of time to find one. Something he would say

or do. It didn't really matter what, she could use almost anything and twist it to her advantage.

Yes, Kate was definitely happy to be back. Who knows, perhaps MI6 and the CIA would really leave her alone in the coming weeks and give her time to read, sleep and see her friends. It would be wonderful, but today's world was big and complicated. China was getting more and more powerful, Russian agents popped up everywhere and Muslim extremists tirelessly continued to plan their heinous crimes. Soon something serious would happen somewhere and then her phone would ring again. She'd better enjoy the time she had with her husband, because before she knew it she would be on a plane again. As Roger sometimes said: 'The free world needs Secret Agent Kate Davenport.'

THE END

COMING SOON: THE NEXT KATE DAVENPORT BOOK

RUSSIAN SPIES IN HOLLAND

(PREVIEW)

ONE

They had been following them from the moment they arrived at Heathrow airport four days ago. Two Russian men in their forties, who were visiting England as tourists. At least that's what it said in their visa applications. After what happened in Salisbury, where two Russian agents poisoned Sergei Skripal and his daughter, alarm bells had gone off immediately in the offices of the British intelligence agencies. So far these two Russians had behaved well though. They visited the sights in London and didn't go off the beaten track once. Nevertheless, MI5 agents David Moore and Becky Pires had followed them everywhere they went. From the Tower Bridge to Picadilly Circus and from Tate Modern to a football match in the Olympic Stadium, where West Ham had played against Crystal Palace. That was the only thing that had been a bit off, agent Moore had thought. On the same day Arsenal played Liverpool and the next day Newcastle came to Stamford Bridge to take on Chelsea. Why did the Russians choose to go see West Ham against Palace in that soulless stadium in Stratford, if they could have gone to Arsenal or Chelsea too? If the Hammers had still played in Upton Park David Moore would have understood. At least that was a real football stadium with an oldschool atmosphere. The other thing that bothered the agents was that, once they were inside the stadium, it had been hard to keep a close eye on the Russians. Sure, there was plenty of footage from security cameras at which people in Thames House, the office of MI5, were taking a closer look now, but with so many people on the move before and after the game, it was hard to cover all grounds. On the other hand it was also tempting to accept that this one little detail was perhaps a bit strange, but harmless nevertheless. Maybe, agent Pires had said, the Russians happened to be lifelong fans of the Hammers, just like those boys in Thailand she had met last year, who were crazy about Brighton & Hove Albion. The world had changed. Nowadays English football clubs had fans all over the world. Agent Moore still wasn't sure though.

On the fourth day of monitoring the Russians, they followed them from Harrods to the Serpentine in Hyde Park, where the two men sat down on a bench and began to feed the ducks, for Christ's sake. Agents Pires and Moore were willing to give it up then. They were three benches away, but had a good view of the Russians.
'Look at them,' Becky Pires said. 'One of them is giggling like a girl.'
Agent Moore still wasn't so sure. He said: 'We don't look like spies either.'
He was right of course. They often worked together, exactly because of that. Petite Becky Pires with the Chinese character tattooed in her neck and chain smoker David Moore in his skinny jeans and Adidas sneakers. Both them were approaching fifty and had worked at MI5 for many years, but a passerby might think they were unemployed and hung out in the park out of boredom. Well, bored they were indeed, but not

because they didn't have a job, but because following these Russians seemed such a waste of time. By now the MI5 agents had started to bet on where the Russians would go next.

'Buckingham Palace,' Becky Pires said. 'That's where they're headed.'

'Haven't they gone there already? Two days ago?'

'No, they were close when they got lost around Trafalgar Square. Remember?'

'You're right,' agent Moore said.

He lit another cigarette and casually glanced over at the Russians, who both had their head turned toward the sun now. Look at them, catching some rays in a park in London.

'I think they'll go get lunch,' he said. 'Fastfood or Italian.'

'No,' agent Pires said, 'sandwiches from Pret A Manger and then to Buckingham Palace.'

'Okay, we'll see.'

Neither of them guessed right. Ten minutes later the Russians got up and headed north to Marble Arch and Oxford Street. The MI5 agents cursed, because there was nothing worse than having to follow someone in a busy shopping street. Thank god one of the Russians was very tall and had a perfectly round bald spot on the top of his head. The other one was shorter, but he was wearing a bright yellow jacket. Another sign, according to agent Pires, that they were just tourists. No spy would be dumb enough to wear something like that, she had said to David Moore a few days ago.

The Russians crossed Oxford Street and went into a Debenhams department store. They wandered around, tried on some caps and seemed to make silly jokes.

Especially the one in the yellow jacket thought he was funny, pulling faces and sticking out his tongue.
'What the fuck,' agent Pires sighed. She had had it by now. Three and a half days of keeping an eye on a potbellied clown from Volgograd and his retarded friend, it was just too much. Therefore her eyes lit up when her phone rang just as they were back on Oxford Street. It was their boss, who first wanted an update and then told her that, as long as nothing was happening with the Russians, he could use her help elsewhere. So agent Pires left, delighted and grinning at her colleague, wishing him luck with boring Pjotr and Igor.
Those were the names that were mentioned in the Russians' passports. Pjotr Rebrov and Igor Sokolov. Pjotr being the clown in the yellow jacket, Igor the tall one with the bald spot. Both born in Volgograd, where they worked as English teachers according to their visa applications.

David Moore continued to follow them by himself. All the way to Tottenham Court Road and from there to Charing Cross. They crossed the street and went into a secondhand bookstore. This made agent Moore suspicious again. What did they want there? The problem was that he couldn't go in to see for himself. He knew the bookstore. It was too small for him to stay unnoticed. From across the street he kept an eye on the storefront while he smoked. At some point the Russians disappeared behind some bookshelves. Five minutes later they came out again and Igor had apparently bought a book which he carried in a plastic bag. False alarm most likely. After all they were teachers and teachers bought books.

Next the Russians headed for Covent Garden. Dammit, agent Moore thought, that's what he should have said to Becky Pires when they were betting on the next destination. A minute later he shook his head in disbelief when the Russians went into a Pret A Manger to buy sandwiches. He took a quick photo with his phone and sent it to his colleague. She would get a kick out of that.

Igor and Pjotr found another bench where they ate their lunch. David Moore yawned, no longer suspicious, just bored and envious of Becky Pires for getting out of this tedious assignment.

The Russians took a look at the Covent Garden market then. They stopped for a minute to listen to a guitar player and when the song was over Pjotr stepped forward in his ridiculous yellow jacket to throw a coin in the hat of the musician. Tourists, agent Moore thought, they're just tourists.

From Covent Garden they walked to Holborn, the two Russian men and the British agent at a safe distance behind them. Where were they going now? The Tube, agent Moore would bet if Becky Pires were still with him. This time he was right. They took the Central Line in the direction of West Ruislip, but got out at Queensway. Back to their hotel for a siesta probably. Bloody tourists, he thought. All the lazy buggers did was eat, sleep and wander around aimlessly.

The Russians went into their guesthouse in Queen's Mews and agent Moore found a bench a hundred meters away from the front door. He lit up another cigarette and took out his phone to send an update to Becky Pires. Then he checked the latest sports news, looking up every now and then to make sure that he didn't miss the Russians, in case they would come out again. They'd be asleep by now though. Most likely he would be here waiting for at least an hour, possibly much longer. Therefore his surprise was big when the front door opened again after only twenty minutes and the Russians stepped out. It wasn't just that they came out much sooner than David Moore had expected, it was also the fact that they were both carrying their big backpacks that surprised and alarmed him. Where were they going all of a sudden? Back to Russia? No, their return flight was not until next week. Perhaps they were going to Scotland or Wales? Paris perhaps? Or maybe they were just changing hotels? But why check out so late then? Whatever the reason, agent Moore was wide awake again. He followed the Russians back to the Queensway underground station. This time they headed east on the Central Line, in the direction of Epping. So that ruled out Paddington Station, David Moore thought, which meant they were not going to Wales or the west of England. When they passed Holborn station, he realized that they weren't taking a train to the north or Paris either. They would have gone to King's Cross or St. Pancrass for those destinations. The Russians did get out at Liverpool Street Station. Stansted airport, agent Moore thought. A cheap flight to god knows where. He checked the time. Six o'clock. If they were indeed going to Stansted he would follow them till there, confirm their destination and call it in. He could be home by eight if he were lucky.

As the Russians entered the busy central hall of the train station, David Moore kept a close eye on them. They looked at a screen with departure times and then walked over to a machine to buy their tickets. David Moore had to wait and pray that he would have enough time to buy a ticket too. When the Russians had their tickets, they headed for platform six. David Moore checked the departure screen. Platform six, that train wasn't going to Stansted! It was going to Harwich. What the hell? Harwich? That could only mean one thing: they were taking the ferry to Holland. What to do now? Make the call and go home? Let the Dutch deal with it? Or go to Harwich as well? He took out his phone and tried to call Becky Pires, but there was no answer. Probably busy with something else. He made a snap decision then and bought a ticket to Harwich too. It was too soon to give it up, he felt. He hurried to the platform and found a seat ten rows behind the Russians. When the train departed he called his colleague again to tell her what was happening. This time she answered and apologized for not responding earlier. He brought her up to speed and she agreed that something suspicious was going on indeed. It just didn't make sense to leave London all of a sudden to take a rather expensive ferry to Holland. It might have been different if they had taken a cheap flight to Amsterdam. In that case the MI5 agents would have concluded that the Russians were going to Amsterdam for some days of mischief and that would have been it.

They talked about what to do next. The ferry was leaving tonight at eleven o'clock and now it was half past six. The train would arrive in Harwich at half past eight. Check-in for the ferry, Becky Pires said, started at eight o'clock. On her laptop she booked a ticket for her colleague and sent him the confirmation email. She also rented a car for him in the Hook of Holland, the port where the ferry was arriving tomorrow morning. Just in case, she said. There was also a train station, she had discovered, so if the Russians were taking the train she would cancel the car. She promised to contact their boss as well. Going abroad on a mission complicated the situation. Becky Pires and David Moore worked for MI5, the British Security Service that focused on interior affairs. Most likely their boss would inform MI6 right away, as they normally handled all things abroad. Agent Moore thanked his colleague and told her that he would keep her posted. After ending the call he sat back and looked at the countryside of Essex passing by. The train made several stops, but the Russians stayed in their seats all the way until Harwich.

At the ferry terminal David Moore kept his distance once again, eating a sandwich and smoking a cigarette while he let the Russians check in first. He felt more relaxed now, because there was no way he was going to lose them on the ferry. What happened tomorrow morning when they arrived in Holland, well, that was to be seen later.

The ferry wasn't too busy, agent Moore noticed. Mostly truckdrivers and tourists, ninety percent of them people from the Netherlands who had gone to London for shopping and sightseeing. The engines began to hum at ten and an hour later the ship sailed out of the port of Harwich. Becky Pires had booked him a cabin with a twin bed, bathroom and tv. He took a shower and then lay down on the bed to watch the news. At midnight he was sound asleep. When he woke up hours later and looked out the window, the ferry was already moored at the dock in the Hook of Holland. It was raining and there was not much activity yet.

TWO

Around the time when agents Moore and Pires were following the Russians on Oxford Street, Kate Davenport was just a few blocks away in a lunchroom on Bond Street. She had been shopping all morning and almost arrived late for her appointment with Jasmine, her Canadian friend, who was already seated at a table in the back. The two women hadn't seen each other in a while, so the first half hour of the conversation was spent on catching up. Jasmine was married to a stockbroker. Both she and her husband were of Chinese origin.
They had moved recently, Jasmine was telling Kate now, because they were planning to have children. When her husband had come across a brand new penthouse in the Docklands they decided to buy it. Kate listened and asked the appropriate questions, but the truth was that talk about babies and real estate usually bored her. Jasmine asked about Roger then and their home near Holland Park. How many square meters was it again? Were they thinking of selling it some day? When Kate didn't really go into it, Jasmine switched to questions about her job. Did she still travel a lot? Kate shrugged and hoped it would suffice to say that too much traveling was very tiring. Jasmine nodded. She understood, she said, but of course she didn't. Like everybody else she was under the

impression that Kate worked for the Ministry of Foreign Affairs. She imagined long flights, stuffy meetings in offices abroad and formal dinners with ambassadors and diplomats. Little did she know that Kate had just come back from Morocco, where she had to kill two men.

They talked about shopping then. A better topic, Kate thought, because it gave her friend less opportunity to be nosy. Besides, both women had spent the whole morning in Westminster, Jasmine in the big shops on Oxford Street, Kate mostly in the smaller boutiques near Bond Street. Each of them had come to the lunchroom with at least three shopping bags and now they opened them to compare what they had bought. Shirts, jeans, blouses and a pair of sneakers for Jasmine. Nothing special, but it made for a nice and superficial conversation.

After lunch, on their way to the Tube, the women went into one more shop. It was a small boutique that sold Italian shoes. It was Jasmine who had seen the shop first, but once they were inside it was Kate who fell in love with a beautiful pair of Casadei pumps. Black and with a four inch heel, they were expensive of course, but when she tried them on, they fit like a glove. Jasmine too seemed to love them, but said the heels were too high for her. Kate bought them and feeling especially happy with her last purchase she was ready to go home now. Tonight they had a dinner party in Chelsea, at Emma's house, her dear childhood friend, and she couldn't wait to wear her new shoes for that occasion. As she was wondering which dress would go well with these heels, they reached the Bond Street underground station. Here Jasmine was taking the

Jubilee Line to the Docklands while for her it was a short ride on the Central Line back to Holland Park.

Roger Winfield, Kate's husband, had forgotten all about their dinner plans. He had a busy week in the City and especially today had been very stressful. So at the end of the day, when the other attorneys proposed to go get a drink to unwind, he decided that that was exactly what he needed too. They went to a pub in Fleet Street and had a few pints. Two at first, but then a third one just before he left. It was only when he was on his way home in the taxi that he realized he had too much to drink and began to worry about what his wife would say if she saw him like this. Hopefully he could make it to the shower without running into her. She didn't like it when he drank too much. It had something to do with an alcoholic uncle in her childhood, who had made a fool of himself at family parties. Roger never met the uncle, because the man had died a long time ago, but he doubted that he had ever behaved like him. It didn't change the fact though that his wife didn't like seeing him in an inebriated state, so he'd prefer to avoid her until he had sobered up a bit.

When he got home he opened the front door quietly, almost like a burglar, and tiptoed up the stairs to the bathroom. He drank half a liter of water from the tap and splashed some in his face too. There you go, already he was feeling more in control of himself. Now a quick shower. He kicked off his shoes and took off his shirt. Then his trousers too, but when he wanted to step out of them he almost lost his balance. Holding on to the sink he told himself to slow down and followed up on that insight with a loud burp.

'God...' his wife's voice behind him said. He looked up and saw her in the mirror, the long, dark hair framing her beautiful face, but her eyes were on fire.
'You forgot the dinner party at Oliver and Emma's,' Kate said. 'And you're drunk.'
'Oh shit,' he said and began to stammer some half hearted explanation. She just shook her head though and turned around. He tried to think of something to say that would make it better, but she wasn't interested. She walked out of the bathroom and down the stairs. Roger looked at himself in the mirror and cursed. How could he have forgotten? Emma was Kate's best friend and even this morning she had said that she was looking forward to seeing her. But wait! He looked at his watch and saw that it wasn't even seven yet. Weren't they expected there at half past seven? There was still time then. Hurriedly he got dressed, but then smelled his shirt and stumbled into the bedroom to take a fresh one out of the closet. Other trousers too, now that he was at it. His socks, mustn't forget to change them as well. In the end he also put on another pair of shoes, but then he was ready to go. When he came downstairs Kate was on the couch watching TV. Christ, Roger thought, she looked gorgeous in the sleeveless black and white top with the turtleneck. Her legs were bare and tanned and a big part of her right thigh was visible because of the split in the black pencil skirt. God, he loved that skirt. And wait, were those new shoes? He pointed at the silver colored heels and asked if she had bought them today. She didn't even bother to reply.
'Are you ready?' she asked instead.
He nodded.
'Let's go then. The taxi is waiting.'

All the way to Chelsea he felt like an idiot. He tried to apologize several times, but she wasn't willing to forgive him yet. Also the beer didn't sit so well in his stomach and when they were almost there another burp escaped from his mouth. Kate shook her head in disgust. He reached out to her then, placing a hand on her knee.

'Kate, listen,' he said.

'Don't you start, Roger Winfield,' she replied firmly. 'And take your hand off my knee, before you make a ladder in my tights.'

Only now did he realize her legs weren't bare, but that she was wearing very sheer pantyhose, as he usually called them. As inebriated and bad as he felt, the realization awoke the fetichist inside him. Kate saw it too and said: 'What? Are you looking at my tights?' Roger felt himself blush. Normally, when they were getting along, they had fun with his kinky preferences, but now that she was angry with him and addressed his fetish, he felt ashamed.

'You're not touching my legs again,' she said. 'Not tonight and perhaps not even until next week.'

She leaned forward and told the driver it was the building up ahead. As Roger paid for the taxi, Kate got out and walked up to the front door alone. She rang the doorbell and while he was still waiting for his change, the door opened and his wife went in. It was going to be a long night in the doghouse, he realized. Perhaps the most worrisome part of it was that his perverted side relished the idea.

TO BE CONTINUED…

ABOUT THE AUTHORS

K.C. Harding is the pen name of a kinky couple from the south of England. Both travel a lot for work and have published several 'normal' travel books. Working on the Kate Davenport series started out as a fun, little project, but more and more time is spent on thinking, plotting and writing.

As the reader will have discovered by now, Secret Agent Kate Davenport is quite the character. Dominant, smart and very sexy she is traveling the world. The first book took place in Morocco, the second will take place in the Netherlands. After that, who knows? Indonesia? China? Or closer to home? Spain or Italy perhaps? And how about South America? There is plenty going on there too now, with a corruption scandal unfolding in Argentina and a Tropical Trump about to win the elections in Brazil. One thing is certain, wherever Kate Davenport will go, she will intimidate the hell out of evil men. She will bring her heels and nylons and sometimes pack a whip too. She will take lovers to bed, for both her own pleasure and the pleasure of her husband Roger who is holding the fort back in London.

Secret Agent Kate Davenport is a natural dominant and that is bad news for some people, but very good news for the rest of us.

Printed in Great Britain
by Amazon